Clemente Chacón

A Novel

José Antonio Villarreal

Bilingual Press/Editorial Bilingüe
Binghamton, New York

ISBN: 0-916950-47-6
Printed simultaneously in a softcover edition. ISBN: 0-916950-48-4

Library of Congress Catalog Card Number: 83-72425

PRINTED IN THE UNITED STATES OF AMERICA

Cover design by Christopher J. Bidlack

Back cover photo by Michael J. Elderman

This book is for my companion in exile,
my beloved son, Caleb,
in whom I am well pleased.

ONE

Clemente Chacón lay flat on his back. His eyes, unseeing, were fixed on the ceiling above him. He had been awake for a long while, breathing quietly, careful lest he disturb the sleeping form beside him. Now he turned and snapped on his night lamp. He picked up his wrist watch, but did not look at the face. Instead, he stared for a long moment at the small calendar on the bracelet. September 1—it was a Friday. 1972.

He switched off the light and lay back again. It was very early for him, but he would not sleep now. The maid would arrive at 6:30. Time enough then to get out of bed.

September 1 . . . or 1 September, as the people at Fort Bliss say, and what kind of bliss could those Army people have at that base? This was *the day*—his day, and Queli's. Queli, who lay sound asleep beside him as if this were not the day it was, as if this was not the day for which he had suffered and waited so long. In repose, she exuded sensuality, that which she repressed, and which he had known only a few times in their married life. On her back, her mouth partly open, her legs parted, she waited for him in a manner she would not when she was awake. He was very much aware of this, and not vaguely, but his mind shifted, because this was also Pete's day. Pete, six years old, asleep in the other bedroom. Suddenly, Clemente was nearly overwhelmed by his happiness. He wished to wake everyone, to shout, to sing, "This is the Day! I am 28 years old and have worked 20 years for today!" But he did not. Carefully, he slid out of bed and went into the bathroom. He sat on the commode, remembered suddenly the times when he had to go into a nopalera to perform this function, then looked at the face on the cover of a weekly news magazine. The face seemed to return his look—youthful, almost supercilious, mod haircut, baby fat evident along the cheekbones. He had read the article. Rags to riches, success story, work, ingenuity and smarts—the American dream achieved in the American way with just enough ruthlessness, Clemente knew, because all that was necessary for this man to achieve his goal, no matter how All-American he looked. Bachelor of Science, business; Northwestern, 1969. Impatient, *the hell with grad school!* Clemente hated him for a moment, then reverted to his old pattern of speech. "Hell, I done good myself! Took me a little longer, maybe, but I don' got no college. Shit! Got no high school!" He uttered the words aloud.

On his way back to the bedroom he stopped to look at his son. "Hi, Pete," he said softly. "How you like Daddy to be on the cover of a magazine?" The boy did not move.

"Why the hell not," Clemente thought, as he eased himself back into bed. "We have a Public Relations director in New England sitting around with his finger in his ass. Good for the Company. Image goes up a notch. All this talk about Chicano Power, Viva la Raza, lettuce strikes, Affirmative Action and here I am, a Mexican wetback with a high school diploma which I stole ... worked my ass off and today I become Regional Manager, four states, of one of the oldest Anglo insurance companies in America ... maybe not one of the biggest, but big enough. Twenty-five K—not as much as that guy in the magazine, but with stock options and bonuses, not bad ... Company rule, nobody under thirty makes more than twenty-five ... wonder why? In seven years, member of the Board? Gotta be thirty-five for that, like the President of the Yew Ess of Ey. Gotta think about that. Gotta keep thinking about that, no matter how stupid it sounds! Must talk to Virgil today. Really not that good, but with this minority shit..."

He did not dream; he was quite serious in his thinking. His business sense was, in fact, quite sound and he was annoyed that he had not thought of this earlier. He knew that within two weeks his picture and his story would be all over the country, not on a front cover, perhaps, but certainly in the business section of a national publication. Because it was good business and was good P.R. He, Clemente Chacón, was Horatio Alger, even if he *was* Catholic and brown.

But he was not brown. In fact he was quite fair, and as he passed his hand over his thinning hair, he was for once happy that his father had been a Spaniard. He thought of making coffee, but suddenly felt concupiscence engulf him. He ran his hand over his body under the covers and was surprised. This did not happen often these days. He turned toward his wife, and now he must have her this minute. Yet, he hesitated.

Gently he placed his hand on her body, moved it upward to her breast. She made a sound, not in displeasure, but then turned away onto her stomach. He now placed his hand on her back, moved it downward, murmuring softly, "Wake up, Queli, wake up." There was an urgency now and he moved his hand to her buttocks. She was wearing panties.

He tried not to think, but he felt her rigid under his touch and knew she was awake.

They had joked about the panties. Her chastity belt, he called them. "What is chastitee balt?"

He had told her and she had not believed him. But she laughed deliciously. Yet, that was not true nor was it a conscious thing with her. She simply could not sleep completely nude. And he could never tell her how that wisp of cloth, almost gossamer, was like a steel plate to him.

And it was too late. The real moment had passed.

She had not always been this way. In fact, although his sexual appetite had always been healthy, she had been the aggressor since they began their courtship. She had chosen him when she was twelve years old, the first time she saw him. And it had been he, perhaps because he was a bastard and his mother had been a prostitute, who insisted they wait for sex until they married. And early in their marriage after their son had been born—she called the baby *One*, always One in those years. "Why One?" Clemente asked. "Because he was wan meestake an' we weel not make another wan," she said and laughed—she came home from work one night and asked, "Is it true what they say?"

"Who are 'they' and what do they say?"

"The gorls at the office—they talk, you know, dorty yokes..."

"Dirty jokes." They spoke English usually, because she insisted.

"Yess, dorty yokes. And they say a man and woman do many things together, not only up and down and inside like we do. Is that true?"

"I don't know," he answered. "I have heard the same thing. I suppose it is an American thing."

"It is French, they say."

"I think it is American. They are the ones who say they do it." He had heard at an early age of what women did to men with their mouths. It had not occurred to him at that time that men might do the same thing to women.

And she said, "So. We are American, no?"

It had been awkward, clumsy at first, and they both felt this, but after a time he discovered there was a special part of her that responded, and in that particular moment they knew that they were blessed. He would lie on his back as she straddled his head, sitting on his face until she moved her upper body down so that she could reach him with her mouth. He felt her downy pubis on his chin and cheeks, and smelled her woman's odor strong as he nibbled and sucked on the small penis-like appendage, making her scream in sheer pain as she reached her climax.

But although she was safe from pregnancy, that too gradually ceased. Once he had come home late from his work with two bottles of wine given him by a customer. They talked and drank, she more than he, and suddenly the bottles were empty and she was as she had been and for a while they recaptured what had been lost. But they were not drinkers, for drink was an obstacle in the achievement of their common goal. They drank very little because they needed their energies, their faculties, and every guile they possessed to become American and successful. They were American achievers by choice and design.

Now she snuggled close and placed her hand on his chest, gently rubbing and pulling on the thick mat of hair. She did not know that she could re-arouse him, could now make everything right for him. She only knew her pleasure in feeling him. And she said, "You are angry."

"No."

"Yes, you are being necio, I can tell."

Suddenly he had an urge to cry. He wanted her to know how much he loved her, *how* he loved her. Flashes of women who had been available to him through the years came to his mind...when he sold door-to-door, housewives that he was certain could be had, others more overt, wearing housecoats or see-through garments exposing breast, hip, and thigh. Others still who said unashamedly that they wanted to fuck. He did not feel virtuous that he had never fallen. He was grateful only that she was all he wanted. He yearned for an indication that she felt as he did. He wanted her to take his cock in her mouth, not so that he should come, but to somehow relieve a particular pain he felt and could not isolate. And this was important right now, because today he recognized his success and somehow there was a hollowness to it. He had in his hands a good portion of that dream he sought, a share he had searched for long before he became an American, long before he knew her.

"Don't be a chiple," she said now as she did always. "You know I love you and only you. I don't have to tell you every day."

Her subtle but persistent rejection of him had first made him follow a pattern in their sex life. Eventually she had stifled his passion so that he began to feel incapable, and worse, along the way he came to believe that it was unimportant. Most of the time, he was content.

"Be a doll and make the coffee," she said. Her new speech, he thought. And somehow he resented it. "Nacha won't be here for another hour."

Christ, what could they do in an hour. Dutifully, he slipped out of bed.

"Aló, One," said Queli.

"Aló, dos," said Pete.

Clemente and Queli sat at the breakfast table, having a cigarette; their coffee was black, without sugar.

"Sit down, m'ijo," said Clemente. "We ate. Nacha fixed huevos rancheros."

"Hey Nacha," said Pete. "No me des any of that Messican stuff. Dame cornflakes y peaches y luego un egg y mucho toast." He turned to his mother. "How come siempre me llamas 'one'?"

"Because you are the only one, darling. We could have five, six or sixteen children, but we only want you. See?"

Clemente thought of his mother. And just as suddenly he was aware that something was wrong. Today he should be thinking of now and tomorrow, not of yesterday. Yesterdays held no joys for him. He had repressed his past. On this day, Clemente Chacón would be reborn a second time. Yet, everything seemed to be taking him back.

"We must move out of this house soon," said Queli, "out of this neighborhood."

"Yes, Calixta," he said. He understood. Pete was picking up the speech patterns of the local Mexican kids. His English was always intermingled with Spanish. And this would not do. He must learn English well; in fact, it did not matter, or perhaps it was important that he *not* learn Spanish. After all, he was American-born. Queli rarely spoke Spanish now, except when she went shopping in Juárez, even though she had never lost her accent.

"And don't call me by that name. You know I don't like it."

"Your name is Calixta, you know. Why don't you like it?" She had never told him, but now she said:

"It sounds Mexican." She blushed and looked down at the table. "Call me Queli, OK?"

He stared at her for a long moment. Finally, he said, "OK." Then he added, "Rent the place. Lower the rent if necessary. Tomorrow we look at apartments, swimming pool, the whole works."

"Sauna bath?"

"Sauna bath, bidets, tennis courts. Check out one of Treviño's complexes. Fixtures look like golf balls, lamps look like tees, Goddamn, how American can we become? Maybe I'll take up the game." She lost his irony. "How would you like your husband to be a golfer?" He remembered the question he had addressed to his sleeping son this morning and felt a twinge of shame and guilt he could not understand.

He reflected on this for a moment. "Later, in a year or two, when I know that we will remain here, we'll look for our own place."

"Not stay here? Why not? Where would we go?"

Clemente laughed. "You still have little faith in what I can do, what the Company feels about me. When the home office sees what I accomplish on my own, it won't keep me in a Mexican town all my life."

"El Paso isn't a town, it's a city. And it isn't only Mexican. Lotta people here not Mexican," she said.

"You're right. Not all Mexican but there's a hell of a lot of them. For now I'm gonna have three 'Messican' states and Oklahoma, too. Indians and WASPS, for Crissake! After a while, I could be sent to Los Angeles, lotta Mexicans there. We'll see."

"I'll put an ad in Sunday's paper."

"Good. I gotta go."

"I'll take the other car. I only have to work a couple of hours, then the hairdresser. Gotta look pretty today."

At the door she took hold of him fiercely. "I'm so proud of you! And I love you." He believed her. As he walked out, she said, "I wish you would change your name again. Both your names."

Again he felt a short spasm of guilt. And why? He wondered. For working hard to improve his lot, to do well for Queli and Pete? It took a few minutes to rid himself of his strange apprehensions.

TWO

"Hey so'jer. You wanna fok my seester?" At that moment, Ramón Alvarez, age eleven, cocked his head upward, then spit a glob onto the soldier's boondocker. He then went into a frenzied movement, snapping his cloth back and forth across the shoe.

The words had come from a small boy standing alongside. He was about Ramón's age, was very dark, with straight, black hair. The young soldier looked at him in dismay.

"Whatcha wanna say a thing like that fer, kid?" he asked.

"Okay," the boy said. He had misjudged this one, and he quickly adjusted his attack. "She is not my seester. But she young. Thirteen, maybe! Leetle teets that big," he held thumb and forefinger close together. "Not much hair around pussy, but she do it good for you."

"Quit foolin' wit' me, kid."

The boy would make no mistake now. The soldier was interested. "I never fool, so'jer. Ask anybody about Mario Carbajal. Anyone on the street can tell you I don't fool." He paused a moment, then continued as if reflecting. "Good to do it early in the day, that way you do it again tonight before you go back to the base."

"No, no, kid," said the soldier. "I don't want no trouble."

"Trouble?" the small boy almost shrieked. "What trouble? Private home, her mother there—everything copacetic—and anyway, we pay the cops. Besides, she's a virgin."

"Naw."

Ramón stood near, not understanding a word. "Ten cen', meester," he said. Those were the only words he knew in English.

"Come on so'jer. Gimme a dollar an' you pay three dollars there."

The soldier gave Ramón a dime and then handed a dollar to Mario.

"Vente, Ramón," said Mario. They walked along Avenida Aquiles Cerdán. Ramón still held his dime in one hand, his shoeshine box in the other. As they moved along, Mario suddenly said, "wait a minute," and ran off the sidewalk onto the street. An American was in the process of parking his automobile and the boy began to give instructions. "Come on back, meester, lotsa room, more, more, tha's good." He ran to the front of the car. "Cut it hard meester, come on, lotsa room, lotsa room." He was quickly at the side of the car, opening the door on the passenger side. He helped a woman out. Again moving quickly, he put a 20-centavo piece into the parking meter. "OK, meester. Your car safe here all day. How long you be?"

"A couple of hours, I guess." The man was nervous. He did not know how much he should give Mario for having helped him park, even though he had not needed help. But the boy was not thinking about that.

"OK, have fun," he said. "Lotsa chops, lotsa souvenirs for the lady. Hot day, have a beer. Take your time. I watch meter."

"How much this gonna cost me?" asked the man, now laughing.

"Just gimme change for the meter—a couple of pesos." The man extended a handful of coins. Mario took a quarter, a dime, and a nickel. "OK, I can get pesos, everything will be alright here. You don' worry about your big, beautiful automobile." He placed a hand on the car, then with his finger traced the letters MC on the dusty hood.

"Very dorty, though." As if he just this moment thought about it, he asked, "Hey, meester—you want a wash job? Maybe weeth polish?"

"No. I can run it through a car wash in a minute when I get home."

"So—you don' have to wait for eet. You go chopping, maybe you let the lady chop an' you relax een the burlycue," here he performed an exaggerated bump and grind, "an' your car weel be ready when you feenish. What you say? One dollar for wash, two dollar for wash an' polish. Good hand job, too. No running through water an' brushes."

The man could not resist. "OK, but just the wash. You want money now?"

"I gotta buy some soap an' rags."

He got the dollar.

Mario went back to Ramón and the soldier. "OK, le's go." They walked a few steps and looked into a restaurant. A tall, thin youth of about 16 years mopped the floor. "Epa, Leopoldo," Mario called. He made the Mexican beckoning sign, the arm moving downward instead of up. The young lad came to the door, mop in hand.

"Quiero que me laves ese carro," said Mario. He pointed toward the car. "Pero que quede limpiecito porque le pertenece a un amigo." He gave the older boy a five-peso bill. "Pero 'horita—pronto, eh."

"Al ratito, ya mero acabo aquí."

"Gracias, eh."

"Las gracias a ti, Mario."

14

They walked on. Ramón, against his will, counted. *A dollar from the soldier, that is twelve pesos and fifty centavos; five pesos for the parking—minus 20 centavos—another dollar for the car wash, altogether 30 pesos. He gave that guy five pesos to wash the car. In ten minutes he made almost twenty-five pesos.* He thought this and looked down at his shoeshine box. Two dimes were in his pocket for three hours of following gringos.

At the corner the light changed against them and suddenly Mario was gone again. He took a dirty handkerchief out of his pocket and began to wipe the windshield of the lead car.

The driver, young, blond and surly said, "Vete." Mario refused to hear him. He walked around to the other side, rubbed on the glass, smiled beautifully at the girl and looked down onto her hiked-up skirt, gazing for a moment at her crotch. He knew her immediately. She had never been here. Boyfriend showing her Old Mexico. "Welcome to México, señorita," said Mario. "Enjoy yourself."

"Don't give him a fucken cent," said the driver. "Lazy little bastards are always trying to con you out of money!" But she was already in her purse.

"Oh, honey. He's so cute and so polite."

"Polite, my ass! The little prick is looking up your snatch!"

She was having trouble finding a coin. The light changed and the young man said, "For Chrissake! Roll the window up and let's go!"

"Goddammit! Don't talk to me like that!" she yelled. The traffic cop on his little soapbox waved to them. He blew his whistle. The cars behind began a dinning—claxons sounded from all directions. She said, "Oh, hell," and handed Mario a handful of coins. Mario leaned his face forward almost in the window and said, "You not get laid tonight, Meester. You wanna fok my seester?"

The driver was livid. He opened his door to climb out, but the policeman was there. "OK, Jack," he said without a trace of accent, "move this goddamn box of nuts and bolts."

Mario was back on the sidewalk counting his money. Sixty-seven cents—almost eight pesos. "OK, so'jer," he said. "L'es go get you some trim."

Ramón had been in Ciudad Juárez only a few months when he met Mario. They got along well immediately; yet, at first, the other's manner irritated him. Mario knew too much, and he acted like he knew he knew too much. Ramón did not believe that he was envious but felt a resentment even though he was learning much from his new friend in the business of hustling a life out of this tourist street. Also, he sensed, and this was the first indication he had of an acute intuition within his own makeup, that because Mario was what he was, so much older than his years, there was much more to learn from him. Mario was at once a hustler, con-man, philosopher and psychologist. Mario would never know the terminology; he operated on instinct. He was impressive but he somehow got on Ramón's nerves.

"Look," Mario had said that first day. "Get rid of that goddamn box. No one makes money shining shoes. Look at the ruquitos in the plaza, sixty, seventy years old, still shining shoes. Been shining shoes for fifty years and you know that fifty years ago they earned more money at it than they do now? I carried a shoe-box around for almost six months before I got smart. I had nobody to tell me about it though." And on that very first day, Mario had shown Ramón his genius. "Can you do 'don Pepe'?" he asked.

"Do what? Who is don Pepe?" Ramón was aware that with each exchange of words with Mario he was exposing his gross ignorance of life. He knew don Pepe did not exist but he did not know what or who don Pepe was not.

"Don Pepe, don Pepe," said Mario in cadence, and did not show his impatience. "The noise musicians make when they accompany singers. Don Pepe, don Pepe... Cuatro milpas tan solo han quedado..." He sang the last.

"Mariachis," said Ramón, his inflection almost turning the word into a question.

"No. Not mariachis," said Mario slowly, deliberately. "They dominate the art..." *I know a thing he does not know,* thought Ramón. *He does not know about Garibaldi and the mariachis some who can barely do don Pepe and yet I did not know don Pepe which means he does know more but I have been to the plaza because Chale took me there...* But Mario was speaking, "I speak of those who know not how to play the guitar. Those who can merely strike those two chords. TA-ta-ta, TA-ta-ta, TA-ta-ta. You know, listen, DON pe pe, DON-pe-pe"

"Yes," said Ramón. He must show him that he was not stupid. "I know now," and he struck a pose as if he had a guitar in his hands and fingered the imaginary strings with his left hand, while his right hand moved across his belly striking the instrument to the meter of don Pepe.

Mario grinned. "Perfect. Let us go." They stopped at a nearby shop. "Don Doroteo," asked Mario, "¿me cuida mis calcos?"

"¿Cómo no?" The old man answered with a question. He would have asked the boy why he wished to leave his shoes, but he knew Mario would merely smile and say nothing.

As they walked up the street, Ramón found it strange to see Mario walk in his bare feet. Mario did not walk like someone unaccustomed to going on bare feet, yet Ramón had seen him a number of times before he met him and he had always worn shoes. Ramón had owned one pair of shoes in his short life, and they had lasted until he came North. Before that, he had worn huaraches, which was very much like not having shoes at all. He wondered why his new friend was doing this, but he would not ask. They stopped at a taxi stand. In a kiosk-like structure a dispatcher manned four telephones. His voice and bearing did not hide his importance; he controlled four telephones, he controlled movement.

"Oye, Mateo," said Mario.

"Me llamo Gertrudis," said the man.

"Ya sé. Pero pa' mi eres Mateo por pendejo." The young boy smiled at the middle-aged man.

Ramón wondered what had occurred between these two. He had not been alone in the streets of the city long enough to have forgot his simple manners. It was not proper that Mario be this disrespectful to an older person, yet he was aware that Mario had a sense of power because the man flushed and mumbled unintelligibly and Mario said, not as a request but almost as an order, a demand: "Tell me when you send someone toward the Chamizal."

Gertrudis merely nodded and did not look into Mario's eyes. And then they were in a cab, riding east, and Ramón accepted the fact that he would never know.

"You want to go to the airport?" asked the driver. "After all, it is a free ride."

"No—just near the Chamizal. We have to catch a bus," said Mario.

"The trip is for nothing," the driver insisted. "Gertrudis said to take you anywhere on my way to the airfield."

"No."

"The divorce airship from New York will arrive soon. A good chance to pick up some change. Some boys make as much as five dollars in propinas..."

"I have heard," said Mario. "I have also heard that some make as little as nothing and even when they make a little they lose it. I have no business there. The bigger boys would take my money."

They rode beyond the strip of land called the Chamizal and were dropped off near the new bull-ring, where there were a few shops and a restaurant for the American aficionados and two or three rundown motels for tourists heading for the interior.

Ramón said, "I would have liked to see the airport and the big airplanes."

To Mario it was incomprehensible to go somewhere strictly for pleasure. "It isn't safe. No one there to protect us. I never go beyond this place, except sometimes when I'm sure it's safe, I take someone to a house out there," he waved an arm in the direction of Mexico City.

"What is out there?"

"Drugs. Just like a gasolinería. They shoot up right in the place. I have never been inside the place. In fact, I never get out of the taxi."

Ramón thought this over. This was something else he had to know about. He knew about mota because his mother had warned him that the vice would eventually kill him if he indulged. He had even seen the handrolled weed because his mother and her friends used it. Shoot up? He did not know, but he would find out. There were some questions he would never ask Mario.

They crossed an empty lot, and Mario went down on his haunches and rubbed dirt on his hands, then sat and did the same to his feet and ankles. His face was already soiled, the uniform of his trade. Ramón looked at his own hands and then at his feet. They moved on and entered a shop filled with metal jewelry, silver and copper, and some made of glass, and there were lamps and dishes, and pottery and clothing, all made by artisans somewhere in the republic and brought here for the Americans. The proprietor, watching his stock carefully, followed them through the store until they came out onto another street where Mario talked to a group of boys milled between a parking area and a mercado sobre ruedas. The boys waited for the residents of El Paso who came here to shop, and helped them carry their groceries to their cars. "¿Le ayudo?" they asked the Tex-Mexes; "He'p you, meester?" they asked the Anglo-Americans. They earned a few veintes in this way, perhaps as much as two pesos a day.

Mario spoke to a boy who wore a New York Yankee baseball cap. "Préstame la cachucha," he said.

"Seguro," said the boy, and handed his cap to Mario, who arranged it on his head.

"Vámonos," he said to Ramón. They walked to a corner and sat on the sidewalk, their legs extended in the street before them. Cars drove by, inches from their feet. "It would be better if I had a guaripa so I could look like a campesino," said Mario, fingering the bill of the cap. "But this is better than holding out one's hand. That is like begging and I will never be a limosnero."

Ramón was patient. He did not know what they were to do. He only knew that Mario should not be questioned. There was a pattern to what was taking place, there was an order to Mario's planning. Looking down at his feet on the pavement, he knew almost as if he had known it forever, that Mario would be with him all his life. And so he waited until Mario spoke.

"Do you know any songs?" asked Mario.

"No."

"It does not matter. Only do 'don Pepe' like I showed you. Get on the bus and to the back and when I signal you, do 'don Pepe' with your phantom guitar. I will sing."

Ramón did not ask about the fare. He simply climbed on the bus. Mario spoke to the driver, and went back to join him.

"Orale," he said, and began to sing. Ramón held his imaginary guitar, but Mario went through two verses before he began to chant "don Pepe" almost inaudibly. Instinctively, he suddenly became a part of Mario, for he heard the other boy's voice, adolescent, almost feminine and beautiful, drown out every street sound; a sudden quietness filled the bus as Mario sang about a youth saying goodbye to his friends, then to his girl and finally to his mother because he was leaving to fight for his rights, his country and his faith. A sentimental song about World War II, a Mexican-American youth going off to win the Medal of Honor for his country—America. And Ramón did not know that the bus had stopped, the driver had turned off the motor, and that everyone was looking at him and Mario because his eyes were blurred so that the tears finally wet his cheeks. He had not been prepared to hear Mario sing like an angel but he should have suspected as much, and then he ran his arm across his face and could see women crying before them and suddenly was forced to catch up his "don Pepes" because Mario now began to sing about a young bracero on a train for California—a world away—to work in the fields, having left his loved ones behind in the barrios of Mexico City, knowing that those who went to that far unknown never returned. And now cries were audible and Ramón knew that it was not only the words, the sadness of the tale, but Mario's voice that had transformed the busload of people and Mario was finished and said in a clear, loud voice, "Hora, todas esas personas que queran cuperar...," and followed Ramón up the aisle with the New York Yankee cap held upside down before him.

Mario did not count the money until the bus was gone. They each

19

had over seven pesos. Ramón was amazed that Mario showed no emotion, either for the amount of money earned or for the manner in which he had earned it. He shuddered slightly. He had known only one person with such an impassive look; he had seen him in darkness, but he had looked upon his face and remembered him well. The look did not show cruelty; he knew cruelty, for his grandfather was cruel, if he yet lived. Here was a complete, total lack of feeling and he was frightened. He was finally forced to ask a question.

"Why did you do that?"

"Do what, loco?"

"You know what."

Mario laughed. "That was the only way to make some pesos instead of a few centavos. They feel sorry for themselves and they are mothers, so they think they feel sorry for us. You and I should know about that."

"I do not understand."

"Well, I do not have a mother, but you still do. But I remember my mother and she lived the life yours still does. The only kind thing she did for me was to get me a shoeshine box—yours did the same for you." He thought for a moment, perhaps with tenderness or yearning, but he did not show it. "They are not wrong though, you know."

"What do you mean?" Ramón felt shame that Mario should know about his mother.

There were no doubts in Mario's mind. The words "perhaps" and "maybe" were not in his vocabulary. He knew everything before his tenth birthday. "Everyone," he said, "must look out for himself. Mothers more than others. And they must do those things. Anything to survive. Once I was in a cantina. This was when I was shining shoes. I was five years old, I remember, because I was told it was my birthday. We were not allowed in cantinas because we would disturb the customers, but we went in on hands and knees under the tables, like little cats we were, a gatas, and if we found a client before we were caught, everything was alright because a customer is a customer. I found one that day—a Mexican from the other side. He was important, I knew because he told me he was an important man on the other side—a lawyer, or something—and I looked up and saw a sign on the wall and wondered, and then I asked him to read it to me. He said that it was in English so I told him that he could tell me in Spanish. On that sign were ten laws how one could protect himself. I only remember one. It was, Tell them nothing! That is a good one. Jijo, is that a good one! But that is the only one I remember. I remember, though, that a guy named Ortega wrote them, a Mexican in the U.S., and it was funny that he wrote them in Spanish and this man had to translate what had been translated from Spanish to English back into Spanish. I finished shining his shoes and I took his hand and asked him to take me to the door because the waiters would kick my ass when I left, and at the door he told me, 'Learn to read, chamaco. Learn to read.'

"You noticed that on the bus there were mostly women. That is why we went all that way to catch the bus coming into town. They have a few centavos to spend on the way to the mercado and the centro. Sing sad songs or religious songs for women—only they might not like it if I sang a religious song because a bus is not a church or even a home, see?"

"But why did you not cry?"

"Because today it was not necessary to cry. Sometimes it is, and then I cry like a waterfall, but sometimes it is not."

"You feel nothing?" asked Ramón.

"I feel only the seven pesos I have in my pocket," said Mario.

This morning Mario had told him to rid himself of his shoeshine box, but Ramón still held onto it. Although he had been shown, he did not truly know how much he could learn from Mario. Also, his mother had paid money for the kit, and he did not know the idiom nor the ways of the street. He had nothing else.

Now, as they walked with the soldier, he felt with his hand the two dimes in his pocket, then gently placed his box against a building. He would never turn back.

Later, they sat on a cement wall at the foot of the bridge. Across the river they could see the tall buildings of El Paso. Downstream on the other side, they saw broad boulevards, automobiles and a shopping center.

"I wonder what it is like over there," said Ramón.

"Same as here. I go there sometimes. Very much work. I worked for one week in the patio of a man there. Patios there are out in front and all around the house into the back, not inside like here. I worked with another one from this side, a guy about thirty years old, and after a week, he got a hundred pesos and I got fifty. I never worked there again. Over there they pay you for your age and not for how much work you do. Very much money over there, but I do better on the street. Women go across and work in houses. They get as much as a hundred and fifty pesos a week. I don't like it over there."

"I think that someday I will live there," said Ramón. He knew at this moment that he would, although he did not know how he knew nor why he should even want to live there. He thought of his migration. He had begun in a small village in the North, an overnight trip on the train from Mexico City, distant enough so that he perhaps would never have known the capital had his mother not taken him there to live. Now he had traveled almost 3,000 kilometers and was here at the very end of Mexico, and how much farther would he go?

THREE

It was very early, perhaps not four in the morning, and the wind coming from the West into the bajío where the buildings of the colonia stood struck him full force as he went outside to urinate. He turned away from the wind to do what he had to do, and he heard the noises of those around him. He knew his mother was at the metate and his grandmother was torteando. The dog, Campeche, came up, and he reached a hand out to touch him. Across the open space and to the left, his greatgrandfather swore mighty oaths; the cows would not move out to be milked. A rich man, his greatgrandfather—he had seventeen cows and each gave three liters of milk daily. Yet, Ramón had never tasted other than human milk in his young life.

Inside the house he sat on the dirt floor with an uncle two years older than he, and he chewed on his tortilla and nibbled on a piece of cheese. Now and then he sipped from a small cup of water. His mother stuffed his morral with tortillas and cheese, he filled the old tequila bottle with water and looped the piece of twine holding it over his shoulder, and with his uncle, walked out into the cold. Every part of him was cold except for his feet, although he had never worn shoes in the five years of his life. Perhaps because of it.

They walked then, he and his uncle, with the seventeen cows, to spend twelve hours in the prairie while the animals grazed, watching that the cows did not stray and most importantly that they they did not leave ejido land to graze on private property because they could be confiscated until his greatgrandfather paid an indemnity, and as they moved away toward the southwest, the sun burst through the horizon on the 8,000-foot high plateau. They fought the winds that struck them and for a moment he stood on a rise, facing the giant red disc on the top of the world. He looked back and on another rise, still in shadow, he saw the women of the colonia, in silhouette, walking in twos and threes into the prairie to defecate—they were but forms, without substance, and throughout his life, when he thought back to this, they would remain without substance even though he knew his mother was one of them, and they became less real in his mind because the years destroyed their living, their having lived, and as he gazed across the plain, the sounds came strongly from the wind sweeping across the sere land.

Today will be different, thought Jesusita as she entered the one-room adobe where she and her son, her brothers and sisters, her father and mother all lived and ate and slept. Her mother and father still maintained a marital intimacy; her mother, in fact, would deliver again in a few weeks. And why not, thought Jesusita. Her mother was young, only 33, and she did not know because she had never seen women outside the colonia and in the village of Cañitas, ten kilometers distant, that her mother had the face and body of a fifty-year old. She had no way to compare. Jesusita was nineteen and her son was five. Juan Ramón Alvarez she called him, giving him her own father's name because she had never had a husband.

It had been in this way.

She was ten years old when don Cayetano Hadad arrived at la colonia. He was of Arab blood, a native of Extremadura in Spain, a region even more dead and remote than this central plateau, yet a region that had sent the conquistadores. He had come to Mexico as a young man at a time when it was possible to gain citizenship and thus to own land. He became a citizen, then went to the United States where he married a young Spanish immigrant and raised his family. He lived there for thirty years and when his wife died he returned to Mexico. Don Cayetano was sixty-five years old when he arrived in the colonia called Los Caballos. And he was robust. He came to the colonia to buy a piece of the earth that reminded him so much of his homeland, to which he could never return because he could not be a part of Franco's Spain. He had some money and a pension, and when he paid in cash for several hundred acres of land and a house with out-buildings, the people knew he was rich. He hired a peon and together they broke a few hectares and they planted beans and corn and every month he cashed two checks— one from the AFL-CIO. At first he cooked for himself and hired a woman to wash his clothing, and eventually he found a girl to cook and keep his house clean.

Jesusita's grandfather became friends with don Cayetano because they were of an age, both older men, and because it behooved him to do so, and when she was thirteen years old she went to work for the foreigner. She was already beautiful, had changed from an extremely pretty girl to a lovely young woman, and she knew how to keep house. She was there early in the morning to fix his breakfast and remained

24

until early afternoon, leaving after she fixed him his noon meal. She would return at five and remain until eight or nine, at which time don Cayetano walked the few hundred yards to her home with her.

The older man was always good to her and always courteous. He bought a portable radio so that she could have music and novelas while she worked and a propane stove so that she would not have to gather wood for cooking. And one evening, after she had been with him for a few weeks, she reached for his plate when he had finished his meal and he grasped her wrist strongly yet somehow gently, and she looked at him, shook her head slowly from side to side but did not speak. He stood up and took her hand and led her through a passageway into another room where he had his bed. He lay her down and she did not resist. Then he walked her home.

"¡Ya chingamos!" said her father to her grandfather. "¿Pos qué cree, don Manuel? ¿Cómo se le hace el negocito este?" He brought out the jug of alcohol to brace their tea.

She lay on her pallet in a corner against the wall and listened. She glanced at the doorway where her grandfather stood, a large man in overalls, barefoot, not wearing even huaraches. She knew how dirty his feet were without seeing them and she knew his greed although it did not show in his grey-green eyes. She would think back to this moment much later, after she had seen and known the seamiest side of life and would yet remember that her grandfather was the most vulgar person she would ever know. Listening to the men speak, she knew very little other than she could never allow them to use her unborn child to get land or more from don Cayetano. But she was a woman and could do very little except decide she would have no more children, which meant she could never again have a man, but this did not matter too greatly because she did not know how not to have a child. And, of course, she could never marry.

Her grandfather sat on the bed with her father, drinking alcohol and epasote. His daughter, Jesusita's mother, filled his cup again and returned to her chores. An infant cried suddenly, and Jesusita's father said to her mother, "¿No puedes hacer callar esa criatura, Rosalba? ¡Con una chingada!"

Her mother brought the child, barely three months old, to Jesusita. Another brother. And Jesusita talked to the child who would not be quiet; by now her grandfather was enveloped in dreams of wealth.

"Oye, Ramón," he said to his son-in-law. "¿A quién le va a quedar todo ese terreno y todos esos animales, eh?" For don Cayetano not only had land but four mules and four horses broken to the plow.

Ramón laughed. "¡Pero qué suerte!" he said. "¡Pero qué pinche suerte tan chula!"

"I talked to him," said don Manuel, "to the old man, I mean, and he will recognize the boy." There was no doubt in his mind that great fortune had been granted them. There was no doubt that the child would be a boy. And a boy to don Manuel was worth as much as a mule.

Jesusita looked up. In a moment they would begin on her. Again and again her grandfather had ordered her to go back and serve the old one, but she would not do it. She had not returned since the day it happened.

"Return to the old one, pendeja," her grandfather suddenly shouted at her, "or he will find himself another woman and where will we be?"

She did not speak. They could do nothing with her. In spite of the patriarchal lifestyle, neither the father nor the grandfather could make her do this because although don Cayetano wanted her, he would not allow her to be forced into coming to him. She was not angry and held no malice toward don Cayetano; she did not fear him, she simply knew she did not want to become his woman, which was what her father and grandfather wanted and which she would be if she returned to work in his house.

She looked down at the child again and suddenly uttered a scream of horror. She jumped up and went to the opening of the choza where there was more light and screamed again. "¡Mamá, mamá, el niño tiene ojo!"

"¡Ave María purísma!" said the mother again and again, crossing herself even as she moved to take the child.

The infant looked back at them, one eye slightly drooped, the other wide, giving the impression that one had diminished in size. Both women cried in fear and don Manuel walked over and felt the child. The fever was there and almost at the same moment, the vomit came.

"Who was here?" he asked angrily. "Who came here?"

"The new woman," his daughter answered. "Of the new people who have taken over the Jiménez ejido. She was here."

"Did she touch the baby?"

"No. She admired him but did not touch him."

"¡Vieja hija de la chingada!" he screamed, for this harm was not done to the child but to *him*. The boy was in the plan of things—to tend cows and thus relieve an older boy for field work, until he, too, became of age to follow the plow.

And there was no one in the colonia who knew how to cure mal de ojo.

Juan Ramón was saddling a horse to go for a curandera when don Manuel asked, "How will you bring her?"

"I will hire a libre."

"Are you crazy? We have no money for such things!" Juan Ramón unsaddled the beast. "You are right," he said, although there was money.

"I will ask don Cayetano to take me. Now he is as of one of the family," said don Manuel in a voice full of confidence. But when he spoke to don Cayetano, he did it humbly. "My grandchild is very ill, don Cayetano, and we need a woman who can cure the malady of the evil eye. Will you take me in your camioneta? I shall pay you, of course," knowing he would never pay.

"Bring the child quickly," said don Cayetano. "We will take him to the railroad doctor."

"No," said don Manuel, now asserting himself. "Doctors do not know about these illnesses. They belong to us. We must bring a woman who knows about these things. There is such a one in town."

"I do not believe in such thinking," said don Cayetano. "Perhaps because I lived in America for so long. The creature should be seen by a medical doctor."

"This *is* America," said don Manuel.

"Let us not waste time on a trivial argument. I know this is America."

Don Manuel showed no anger; he was no longer humble. It was rare that he should do this before a man whom he knew according to his own beliefs to be superior to him. But don Cayetano was interfering in a matter that was not his concern. "I will never," said don Manuel, "allow one of those you call medical doctors to even come near one of mine!"

Although don Cayetano was aware that he had intruded, he was surprised at the vehemence and manner of don Manuel, but he knew these people, not much different from his own in Spain, and he also knew that he could never understand them. He said, almost sadly, looking into the other man's almost green, pig-eyes, "I think then we should be on our way."

On the road, don Manuel placed his hand on the other man's arm. He did not think it strange that this man, a bit older than he, was the father of his unborn great-grandchild. But he did think of the fact that they were already connected, and for that reason he did not want to alienate one that was to be a benefactor. He apologized.

"Forgive me that of a moment ago, don Cayetano. It is that you are new here and you are rich. For us, the peonada humilde, things are different. They can do anything they want to do to us."

"They?"

"The doctors, the lawyers, the teachers, the priests, the government. And they are all the Government. The lawyers, now, we all know what they are even in foreign countries where you have lived. The doctors and teachers here are of the Government. The teachers are not people to have in your house. The doctors teach the women bad things; the teachers teach our children bad things. They are all communists, and they do not believe in God. I am proud to say that not one of mine has spent a day in school and not one has been to a doctor. And the priests, although they are with God, and it is said that they are outside the Government, are really in league with it. Everything is set up to fuck up the campesino. The priests, by their example, show us that there might not be a God, and the Government folds it twice before it sticks it into our rectum. It gives us a few hectares to work although It really owns the land, land full of rocks. And in a three-year drought when we have no crops, the priests tell us it is the will of God and the Government says, 'Plant *your* land; show initiative!'" Don Manuel's voice was almost a whine. "And then the Government sends professors to teach our children disobedience and heresy. It sends soldiers to vaccinate our animals so that they will die and make the price of the rich people's animals go up. And now they are sending doctors to do the same to our children. Vaccinate them as if they were were animals, to make them sterile because there are already too many Mexicans! Too many Mexicans! Look, it is ten kilometers from the colonia to Cañitas and there is not one family between here and there. Look to your left, the Tetillas, perhaps thirty kilometers away, and there is no one there—the llano is open, and they say there are too many Mexicans! And they talk to our women and tell them that they should refuse to cohabit with us, the men, because there will be more children and the priests come and say, do not listen to the Government, it is the Devil incarnate, broken up into many men and now some women. The will of God is what matters and God says women are on earth to have children, they were created specifically for that purpose, to people the earth. And they are confused, of course, but there is nothing they can do about this confusion. We are men and we cohabit. And one thing is not understood by these people who come to us. We *need* children to survive—male and female children we need in the very same way we need water and good land, otherwise we will simply disappear from the earth. And our women care only because they give life to children. They do not enjoy the act the way we do; you should know that my granddaughter did not experience pleasure in what you did with her in the same manner that you did. But now there is a boy and he tends cows and she is fulfilled because she is a mother and one day he will be behind the plow and then, when he is eighteen or so he will marry and then I will have another woman in the house to help make cheese, to gather wood. And these people, without offense, including you, come here to change our ways. We have lived this way forever—my father, my grandfather, his father and his father's father— we have always lived in the manner of our people. And we *are* here, therefore it must be the right way to live. It *must* be the right way to live because that is the way la gente does."

Don Cayetano wondered. *This man thinks!* He is not the mere brute I have thought him to be. And are they really gente? Yet, there is logic in his thinking from his point of view—even though he is wrong because the word "progress" and the word "change" are abhorrent to him. He is wrong through his ignorance, and he is ignorant because he and his generations have been taught to be ignorant . . . there is so much I do not know about them and *my* people taught them what they know from the very beginning. A mongrel race it is said, these mestizos, and I suppose we are responsible.

And don Manuel, still caught up in his wrath against the interlopers, spoke. "How in the fuck can there be too many people in Mexico? Look into the prairie. Do you see anyone? You can go leagues into the prairie and sometimes not see one person. Too many people!"

The man was repeating himself and don Cayetano wished he could explain to him how wrong he was. But at this moment he was not certain don Manuel was wrong. And he did not want the conversation to continue because he felt a guilt and knew not why. Certainly he did not feel guilt about the girl; perhaps the feeling was because he was Spanish, and the Spaniard helped create this creature. Then again, he should not have guilt because of this man's ignorance. He, don Cayetano, was not poor and lived among poor people. Perhaps that was the cause of his discomfiture. Nevertheless, this guilt forced him to defend his position even though he did not know why he must.

"Take the rocks out of the labor," he said. "Dig wells. This is the good earth." He knew his mistake immediately. He was telling don Manuel he was poor because he did not work, and he knew this was not true.

"Wells, even those we could dig by hand, require pumps. You have a deep well and a turbine, for you are rich. Would you give us water?"

"You know I cannot give you water. I can only move water into your ejido on an hourly fee. It costs money to pump water, you know."

"I know," said don Manuel. "I thought you did not know."

Both men were silent as they bounced and bumped on the goat trail. He is so right, thought don Cayetano. Even this, not a graded road to be found for the people to get into town to bring whatever greens and grain they could beat out of this arid land. But *he* had worked for what he had, he also knew, worked for years during the great depression in America, raised his children, and but for the fact that he no longer needed to hire out his services, he worked even at his age.

They returned to the colonia after midnight. The child was comatose. Its temperature had climbed and its body twitched spasmodically. The woman they brought with them handed a small can of olive oil to Jesusita and told her to warm it. She then mixed lard and salt, kneading the substance with her hands until she was satisfied with the consistency.

She asked, "Do you know who the person is?"

"Yes," answered Jesusita's mother.

"Have someone see that she remains awake. I want to know when her headache comes." She undressed the small body then and rubbed the lower torso including the feet and between the toes with the salt and lard mixture. When she was done, she cleaned her hands and gently rubbed the upper part of the body with the warm oil. "The egg," she said and it was handed to her.

"Is it fresh?"

"Tonight's," said Jesusita.

The woman crossed herself and began to pray. Slowly she recited three paternostros while she moved the egg over the entire body of the child, careful to touch the skin of every part of him. When she finished, she wrapped the child and placed the egg under the small pillow, arranging it so that it would not be crushed.

She sat at the foot of the bed. "I will have some tea now, if there is some," she said.

"What do we do now?" asked Jesusita's mother.

"Now we wait."

"How long will it take?"

"By tomorrow morning some time. In a few hours the person responsible will have a headache. I want to see her then. I will touch her and bring the touch back to the child. In the morning I shall need a few straws from a broom."

"I shall get them," said Jesusita.

The men went to sleep on the floor as did the children. Only Jesusita, her mother and the woman remained awake. At dawn they went outside to urinate, then the woman asked for a bowl of water. She took the egg from under the pillow and carefully cracked it into the bowl. She then broke the brittle pieces of straw and gently arranged them around the egg until she had formed three crosses. The bowl was then placed under the bed, directly under the child's head.

"It is done," she said. "When the egg cooks, the eye will resume its normal size and the child will be well."

The cows had been milked and the boys were off into the prairie with them. The men stood outside the hut smoking, waiting. Inside there was a stillness. Occasionally, the women looked under the bed, but the bowl was never touched.

Once, finally, after looking into the bowl, the woman looked toward the child and concern showed in her face. "The child has died," she said. And screams filled the small hut.

The men entered. "How can it be?" said don Manuel, angry at the woman. "You have experience in these matters."

"I have," she answered. "And I have cured many, but sometimes God does not want it that way. It is His will."

"You did not know what you were doing," he insisted.

"You are wrong," she said, and there was a sadness in her eyes. "Everything went accordingly. The woman had her headache and look at this." She took the bowl from under the bed to show the three crosses still floating in perfect symmetry, while in the center, the egg lay perfectly poached.

"I will not pay you, woman," said don Manuel. "I will not pay you!" They were outside now and don Cayetano was there.

"Come, señora," he said, gently taking her arm. "I shall take you home and I, myself, will pay you."

In a house near the edge of the settlement, another woman cried silently. This was to be a new home for her and her family. And now she knew that for a long time, no woman in the colonia would allow her to look upon her infant.

In all this time, almost six years, Jesusita had not been to the house of the man who had fathered her child, had in fact never spoken to him. But she remembered his kindness, and now that her mind was made up, she would go to him. She knew she had resisted all these years because otherwise she and her son would never escape. She also knew that don Cayetano would help her. She did not know that he, the old man, had been giving her grandfather a few pesos every month to help defray his son's expenses.

She helped her mother through the day, happily. At times she even burst into song. And in mid afternoon, she walked to the house of the old man.

"You came, child," he said softly.

"Yes, don Cayetano." She could call him nothing else.

"How can I help you?" he asked, for she had not returned to stay and he did not really want that now.

"I want money so that my son and I can leave here. He should be in a real school this coming year and he can never go to school here."

"He could go to school in Cañitas," he said.

"My grandfather would never allow it, you know. He needs him to tend the cows. I do not want Ramón to grow up like this." She did not tell him what they both knew; that don Manuel also needed the boy as a means of getting don Cayetano's land.

"He could go to school in Cañitas if you lived here with me," he said, because he would do this without conditions and she would not be living as his woman.

"I cannot live with you, don Cayetano. Forgive me, but I cannot do that," she said.

He nodded. "Your grandfather will be very angry if I help you in this, you understand."

"Yes, I understand. And I will never ask you for another thing as long as we live."

"He believes, and I suppose he has a right in believing it, that what I own will go to our son someday. I have arranged for a part of it to be Ramón's after I die. It will be his legally, and someone will see that he gets it even if he never wants to live here. But it will be his—it will never belong to your grandfather. Also, I will send you some money periodically wherever you go."

"I do not want that. I must simply get away."

"I understand, child," he said. "Where would you go?"

"Everyone who escapes from the town or even from here goes to Torreón. I do not want that. I wish to go to México. I wish to lose myself from my people."

"And when?"

"Quickly. Even today, except the train has passed. Tomorrow. Yes, tomorrow."

"Alright," said the old man. "I shall talk with your grandfather tonight. I shall simply tell him that I am taking you and the boy into town because you both need clothing. He will not deny that and it will not occur to him that you are running away. Also, the boy will need shoes if he is going to México. Tomorrow, you will be on your train."

"Thank you, thank you," she said. And she took both his hands in hers and kissed them.

It had been fun in México with his mother. He was six and she was twenty, and they were more like brother and sister as they walked the streets looking into stores or to Chapultepec to watch the boats, or to the zoo. She had tried for a place with a rich or foreign family so that she could keep her child with her, but she could not cook what they ate, could not really speak their language and knew no one who would recommend her even as the lowest form of domestic.

For a time she worked in a small, greasy restaurant, selling cochinita pibil and tacos al pastor, on her feet all day, but she was young and enjoyed it. One day the proprietor told her that a cousin had arrived from Mérida and he had no need for her services. For a while, she nearly panicked. She thought of her son, for she fed him all his meals in the kitchen of the restaurant so it meant that she lost more than her meager salary.

They lived in Hipodromo, on the roof of an apartment building. The people to whose apartment these quarters belonged did not have a maid, so they rented the room to her inexpensively.

She tried to find work but had no luck; yet by now she knew a few people in the neighborhood and it was not too bad. Down the street, a squat, ugly man had a newsstand. She always stopped to talk to him, for he too was from the provinces, from Huichapan in the state of Hidalgo. His wife, a young woman, was suspicious, but he set her up with vegetables or leftovers from their own fare to help her through. She also had among her acquaintanceships young girls her age, and some a bit older who were prostitutes. Some did it deliberately and some were in the situation that is at once the misfortune and disgrace of México: the unwed mother turned out by her family for her transgression, no hope for marriage, untrained even for whoredom. They visited her, usually in the late afternoon for they slept all day, and sometimes would leave a peso or two on the table.

And since they knew it was inevitable that she would follow their path, they hoped to move her in that direction quickly, but they did not push her.

"Mira, no estés tan triste," they would say. "Ven con nosotros al Bisi Bi nomás para que te diviertas siquiera un ratito." The Busy Bee was a clean, good looking bar in Roma which catered mainly to American students, ex-G.I.'s at Mexico City College on the G.I. Bill. Since classrooms were in buildings all over the colonia, The Busy Bee on Coahuila was very near.

She would laugh and say no. She knew nothing about such things. But although she had had intercourse but once in her life, at age thirteen, frantic, hurried, painful, so nearly totally devoid of pleasure that she would have forgotten it by now had her boy not been present to remind her, she was young, almost stunning in her beauty, and she knew the need she felt. And the first time she accompanied the girls, after Ramón was asleep, nervous about leaving him for an hour or two, she became a professional in that life for which she had been destined from birth. The following night she discovered the palo blanco existed. Her profession did not allow for freelance work.

Her pimp was a pleasant young man. He explained everything to her. "You must understand that you do not work for me. I am merely an employee as you are. This is a sucursal, you might say. Take care of yourself, learn to dress, watch your speech, read, perhaps enroll in a course at an institute. It is not necessary to learn English, but you must drop your ranchera speech patterns. I will watch you, but I do not own you. Once in a while when the urge comes or the need I will take you to my apartment. This is a rare thing."

"What if I say no to all this?" she asked.

"You cannot say no, and you cannot quit. But it is not bad. You will not be bothered, you will not be abused. You will go to a doctor today and you will go to him every month. As I say, this is a branch office. You are beautiful and in six months if you cooperate, we will move you to the Reforma. First a smart night club, then to a house. This is a good place to begin, but it is on the way up or down. All these girls are on their way down. They use drugs or drink too much or they simply were never good enough for the top. This is a big organization. If you wish we could send you to Acapulco or any large city—if you wish also, we could send you to a small village in the center of Zacatecas where you will work as a three-peso whore. It is up to you. Your name, Jesusa Alvarez, is too coarse. You are now Mago Marín. This name has been selected for you with care. If you fail you may have your name back."

She said, and was herself surprised at the sarcasm in her words, "Thank you at least for that." But he did not hear her.

"There is one other place that is within your reach. Few ever get there. It is far beyond the rich places on the Reforma. It is the matrix—a grand estate here within the District. There, guests are allowed to remain for weeks. Its clientele is of the highest caliber. There are foreign dignitaries, lesser royalty, international millionaires. Those of you, the very few who make it there, will never go back down. Famous motion picture stars launched their careers at this place. From there have come more than a few countesses, one actual princess and many of these women have married wealthy men of fine family backgrounds."

Jesusita did not leave her room for two days. She did not eat, and did not worry about her son since there were a few hard bolillos and in a plastic bag hanging from a nail on the wall was a good piece of Chihuahua cheese. There was also water, so he could eat. She still had the forty pesos from her first trick in her purse and she would not touch them, would not look at them. She did not feel dirty and did not really think about what she had done, but looked upon the money as something that had again enslaved her. She had been free for such a short time.

On the following day she suddenly opened her eyes. She knew without looking at her small clock (the only object she had ever bought for herself) that it was quite near dawn. She had spent two days and a few hours mostly in bed. Not quite overcome by lassitude, she knew that today she must get up and use the devil money as she thought of it now, for her son must have nourishment. Suddenly she was happy that she had not disposed of it. She had considered doing just that, giving it to a limosnero, throwing it down a drain. She did not know why she had not done it, because she was unaware that poverty is a handicap, no different from lacking a limb or even a mind; nor did she know that the handicapped will create instincts, survival skills, because the only animals she had known had been domestic.

She walked across the roof of the building, carrying her laundry to the common washtubs. Two maids who worked for people who rented in the building were doing their personal chores before going down to their daily work. She sat down to wait her turn. She was hungry and there was nothing to eat. Her mind was made up. One girl finished and Jesusita quickly washed her things and hung them up. She went for her money and then ran down the six flights of stairs and across the street to the panadería. She bought pan dulce and a liter of milk. Later she would go to the mercado and tonight she would make more money. Now that she knew what she must do, now that she accepted the fact that she had a commodity that was in demand she felt a relief that made her face beautiful once more. She seemed almost happy.

Once she and Ramón had finished their breakfast, she walked out on the roof again. A well-dressed woman stood with her back to Jesusita, looking down over the low wall to the street below. She turned and Jesusita was astonished that a woman that old could look so youthful, be so beautiful.

"I once lived in places like this," said the stranger. "Not only that, I had to work for the pigs who owned them. Whatever happens to you, don't ever be a gata."

She was a women in her mid-thirties. "Armando sent me," she said. "I will be your tutor for a few weeks, then I will take you shopping. And I will take you to a school where you will be taught how to speak."

"Do you work also?"

"Oh no. I did for fifteen years but now I am married. I help out now and then." She knew Jesusita was amazed, and said, "My husband is in the government. It amuses him that I have something to do. I do other things—I work sometimes in orphanages and in clinics for the female diseases, the occupational hazard of our profession. Although I do not work anymore, as I said, the occupation got me where I am and I have never regretted having been a prostitute. I also dedicated a dam once, believe it or not, near a dirty little village such as you and I know so well. I think of myself as an example for you, but you must learn much, above all, self-discipline. There are rules also for those such as we, and morals and patterns of behavior. Now I am a grandmother, if only a step-grandmother, and I am respected. At this moment many men want me, the biggest men in Mexico, and because I am trained in the art I can fuck them dizzy but I cannot do that. I am tempted now and then but it cannot be. That is self-discipline. I cannot do it because I am not a great actress, singer, poet, painter—they could do it without repercussions, but I am simply a rancherita who was fortunate enough to be physically and mentally equipped for a lucrative trade. If I should do that, then I would be back in my village turning two-peso tricks.

"That is the way of this life. You can have the best life if you work at it and remain decent, the worst if you allow yourself to become common. Yet, I admit it is not for all of us. There is a singular characteristic of the macho. He will put his prick into anything that moves until he has money. Then he wants intelligence and beauty with his cunt. In a way I am to find out about your brains. Your beauty was reported long before you went to the Busy Bee."

During this time, Jesusita had remained silent, but in her naive way looked at the woman, and the other, being herself a campesina and a woman, knew the question in the young girl's face. "Yes," she said, "but unlike you, I had two. A boy and a girl. And I have not seen them since they were very young."

36

She was silent for a time. Then she said, "My chofer will pick you up every afternoon. We will begin with table manners. You will learn all the graces. Then we will work on make-up and dress. You must continue to work to pay for your clothes. I come free. Work only from eleven at night until five in the morning except when it is impossible to do it. Arrange to have someone take care of your boy. You will need all your rest."

Now every day Ramón was awakened to the odor of food, frying sausages, fresh pan dulce from the panadería on the corner across the street, fresh papaya or mango—elegant food so inexpensive, yet a short while ago so inaccessible. After his mother slept, they would walk the block and a half to Sanborns for an ice cream soda, or over across Insurgentes for cochinita. She would leave for school then, and later, before she went to work, she would read to him haltingly from a book called *Bertoldo, Bertoldino y Cacajena.* Then they would either go around the corner, again on Insurgentes, for pozole or merely walk up that broad avenue for an elote from a sidewalk vendor or a tlacollo from a shapeless little Indian lady who set her fire right out on the sidewalk and cooked on order. These were happy days for both. And then one morning Ramón woke knowing something was wrong. His mother was not there, but then he looked down from his bed and saw her on the floor with her arms entwined around the body of a red-headed, red-bearded giant.

She had committed the cardinal sin for a whore. She was in love.

FOUR

When Charlie Morgan was growing up in El Paso, he believed that his father was a rich man. The Morgan family lived in a "nice" house in Highland Park, an upper middle-class, all white neighborhood. Charlie had a bicycle, a .22 rifle, and his own room, and Mr. Morgan had no problem making his monthly mortgage payment to the Building and Loan. A veteran of World War I, George Morgan put his thirty years in the "Calvary," and took a job at Fort Bliss. With his salary, retirement pension and the Post Exchange, he sometimes was not even aware there was a depression.

In truth, George Morgan was not very much aware of anything other than his army record, his job and his American Legion Post. The American Legion, he had to admit, was a disappointment. In the Great War he had fought in the Infantry, to be sure, but had immediately rejoined the Cavalry, which refused to accept the fact it was now useless. He defended his country now against the Wobblies in Oregon, and had taken part in the castration of an I Won't Work in the interest of National Security. He also enforced the Volstead Act along the Mexican border even though he enjoyed a belt or two himself. The Legion was at work against all forces of evil that threatened his country, labor unions, foreigners, commonists and sin, and he was proud to belong. But one day he went to a department convention in Santa Fe and got drunker than a lord during pre-convention festivities but not so drunk that he did not realize that someone or more than one kept grabbing at his ass and finally when goosed for the tenth time, he turned around and punched the gooser in the mouth. He learned later that not only was this man a Post Commander somewhere, but he was an ex-Colonel. He was never again invited to join the fun. In truth he did not know that goosing was a favorite pastime of the Legionnaires, along with clubbing poor people on top of the head. Later, during the second big war, when McArthur ordered jeeps instead of horses, the old trooper knew that his country had betrayed George Morgan.

George Morgan was also aware of his family, of course. There were two older boys besides Charlie and there was also a girl, and he believed that his family was living a full, satisfied life. But Charlie Morgan had never been satisfied. He was the youngest and he idolized his older brothers who were well-known high-school athletes. He was something while they yet lived, but they died very early in the new war, almost in the same week at opposite ends of the earth, and it seemed his world ended. When his mother joined the Gold Star Mothers and his father sat in the parlor thinking of how he could re-up at his age while proudly contemplating the two decals on the window, he almost died also. Then his sister married and he was truly alone.

Later, at Austin High, where his brothers had compiled athletic records, he was singularly unexceptional. He was almost six feet tall and full-bodied at age 15. The coaches talked to him, talked to his father, but for once Charlie refused to obey his father's command. The coaches who watched him play on sandlots recognized an innate ability and a remarkable potential, but they did not know that he was intimidated by the reputations his brothers had left, and by the fact that his father had never forgiven him for not being old enough to fight the Hun and the yellow, little Jap. The war had passed him by while his brothers died in glorious battle. He could not compete. He felt inadequate—was inadequate in class, in crowds, in relationships with boys and girls. That year he was fifteen, his father, in an uncharacteristic moment, recognized his son's loneliness. He wrote to an older brother in California. He had not seen him in twenty years, since a time he had bivouacked near San Diego. His brother had settled in a small town named El Cajón. And that summer of his fifteenth year, Charlie Morgan went to El Cajón and those six weeks changed his life.

Micha Morgan left his North Texas dirt farm long before his younger brother, George, joined the Army. Perhaps because he did not like the farm and because the short, successful war of his childhood had made the nation aware of sea power, it had been his idea to beat his way to the West Coast, work at odd jobs for a while, then enlist in the Navy. His first job, however, as a pearl diver in the U.S. Grant Hotel in San Diego, brought him in touch with a slender, young waitress and he changed his mind about the Navy. She was a serious girl, with a strength of purpose despite a wistful look. There was no courtship whatsoever. They both knew and they married.

She had come to San Diego from a crossroads hamlet a few miles east, and so there they went to live. Her father arranged a job for him with a citrus grower, and he remained there for the rest of his life. They were given the use of a small clapboard house in the orange grove, and to this they added rooms as their family grew. Now they had only their youngest, Jody, but their married children all lived nearby so their grandchildren filled the large house.

Charlie Morgan came to a happy home. He sensed it immediately. And Jody, who was eighteen and a recent high school graduate, did not make him feel like a kid. He did not even allow Charlie to express his natural reticence toward social activities, but immediately took him off to a swimming party. While he did not become the life of the party, he did talk and enjoyed himself, and since he was as large as Jody, the others accepted him as being their age.

Later that night, after a family dinner where he met the entire clan and after answering questions and becoming acquainted with his Uncle Micha and Aunt Beth, he and Jody talked.

"You know, Janie Blair liked you pretty much," said Jody.

"Which one was she?" he asked, knowing very well who she was. He felt a catch in his chest as if he had been caught in a secret thought.

"The polka dot, two-piece suit," said Jody, believing Charlie did not remember. "If it's OK with you, I'll get Pam to fix it up so we can do something together."

Charlie knew that afternoon that he liked his new-found cousin. He had never felt as comfortable around others as he had at the party. Because he was aware that here was a kinship he needed very much, he felt he must be completely honest, and he said:

"You got to know something about me, Jody. I'm not really very good at that sort of thing. I liked Janey a whole lot, too, but I wouldn't know what to say..."

Jody interrupted him, "Who in the hell talks on a date, Charlie? Christ!" and he laughed.

"That's just it. I've never been on a goddamn date. I wouldn't know how to act."

"No shit?" Jody did not believe him.

"No shit!"

Jody laughed again. "Man, you could have fooled me. But, hell, that's no problem. I was kidding about not talking on a date. We'll just ride around, maybe go to a drive-in or to the beach if you feel like it. You'll talk, you'll see, and maybe you'll make out OK."

Charlie was frightened and for a moment he was quiet. Then he grinned in embarrassment and said, "OK."

"I'll make the call now, then," said Jody. "We'll go tomorrow night. And don't worry, for chrissake."

He went the following night, and he learned that he could indeed talk, and he saw the ocean for the first time. And Janey Blair taught him how sweet a sixteen-year old tongue can taste, but she did not let him touch her breasts.

"Jesus!" he said to Jody as they were driving home after dropping the girls off. "I'm going to have to wear my jock strap if we do that more often. He was suddenly very self-conscious, and wished he had not blurted it out like that.

But Jody made it just fine by being so natural. "She knows you have a joint, for chrissake. And she knows it gets hard." Again he was laughing, and Charlie was forced to laugh with him.

He supposed it was true. It made sense, but he could not control a sense of shame. He was glad they were in the car and not in the house where Jody could see his face. He wondered if he would always be this way. But he was jolted into near panic by Jody's words:

"You ever been laid?"

He swallowed, choked for a moment, then said in a flat, almost contrite tone, "No." He shivered and felt deep pain in his stomach.

Jody was quiet for a time, then said, "You don't have to feel that way. There's a first time for everybody. I got mine for the first time only last year. Now Pam and I make it regular and I don't even remember how I felt about it when I was still cherry."

Charlie shook because he had nearly lied. Now he was troubled by what Jody had just said. He had heard boys at school say such things, and never really believed, but now he could ask:

"Honest, Jody? Don't kid me because I have to know."

"It's not that serious, man. Sure it's true. It was crappy at first using those goddamn rubbers. Pam wouldn't do it unless—but it's been great since she talked her Mom into getting her a diaphragm. Now she wears it whenever we go out. Not tonight, though, because we were doubling."

"What's it like?" asked Charlie.

Jody laughed. "Jesus, I don't think anybody can tell you that. You'll find out."

"Thanks. I guess I'm pretty dumb—I don't know too much."

"Hell, you're only fifteen," said Jody. "You've got a long time to go." Charlie was silent, and Jody added, "Dad told me your age, but don't worry, I won't tell anybody. I won't tell anybody you're cherry either. Things'll work out, you'll see."

It was hot, but it was a beautiful day as Jody drove on the empty, two-laned backroad toward San Ysidro and Tijuana. Beside him sat Charlie, in the rear three other youths. Charlie knew two of them from the day he had arrived. The third, a large, overweight redhead who could not stop talking was brought along because he was twenty-one. It was he who bought the beer at the country store they had just passed.

It was a lazy ride. Charlie sipped his beer, half listening to the redhead talk about cunt. At least, he thought, taking another drink, beer isn't a first. His father had always allowed him to have beer. Jody had told him he would find out soon, and, boy, he meant it. Here it was, only a week and he was on his way to his first woman. He wondered what she would be like, what she would look like, then he thought again of that which he wished to forget. Since Jody told him yesterday afternoon that they would be going to TJ today, he had masturbated seven times. Five times last night and twice this morning, once in a gas station john, for crissake! So even if he could overcome the fear he felt because he did not know how, he had a fear that he could not do it even if this were the first time. He thought, idiotically, that he did not have a drop left in him. He was sore, but the self abuse did not bother him. In one of the only sage bits of knowledge his father gave him, he had been completely purged of those inhibitions.

"If beatin' your meat makes you crazy," George Morgan had told him, "we woulda lost the war." To him there had been only one real war even after he lost his sons. "I put in thirty years in the Calvary an' troopers was always flogging their dummies an' I never knowed one that wen' out of their head. Mebbe you could do it so much you get to like it mor'n wimmin, but I never seed one what did." He did not know how happy he had made Charlie.

"Let me pick one out for you, Charlie," said the redhead. "I come over here regular, and I know the good ones. Want another beer?"

"Sure," said Charlie. "Thanks."

"He means sure to the beer, you big tub of lard," said Jody. "Let him pick out his own woman, for chrissake!"

"I'm just trying to help him—give him my experience, so to speak. A whore isn't like making it with your chick."

"Only reason Fats goes to T Town so much is because he doesn't have a chick," said one of the others.

They all laughed except Charlie, who suddenly felt sorry for the loud one, but then he realized that the redhead also laughed.

"No more beer for you, shithead," he said in mock anger to the youth beside him. He had not been offended.

Charlie did not know how they got to The Little Red Mill. They crossed the border, went across what seemed like a wide river bed, but it could not have been because dozens of cardboard shacks were built at the bottom and hundreds of children played in the sand. This was not like Juárez, which he knew. There, one was in the city the moment he crossed the border, whereas here the city seemed quite a distance. El Molinito Rojo was separated from the town, looking peaceful and quiet at this time of day, and cool despite the heat because it was shaded by innumerable trees. There was a small house-like structure, restaurant and bar, and a stone walkway led to a huge rectangular building.

The youths went into the bar and sat around a table. They were the only ones there and a waiter was with them immediately.

"Cinco Tecates bien frías," said the redhead. He turned to Charlie. "Gotta ask for 'em cold 'cause these Mexicans take theirs hot, al ti-empo, an' if you don't tell 'em not to, they'll give 'em that way to you too."

Jody shook his head and said, "Christ, Red, Charlie knows as much about Mexico as you do. Don't forget he lives in El Paso." Then, because he felt responsible for Charlie, he called the waiter back and said, "Give us two double shots of tequila." He turned to the others and said, "Charlie always uses beer for a wash—think I'll try it. You guys want some?"

"Hell, no!" they said in unison.

They drank for a time, not talking much, merely enjoying the silence and the beer. "Well, the hell with this ol' shit," said Red. "I'm gonna take care of my business. I like it here this time of day. They don't rush you through an' they're not sloppy from all them other guys that come before. You guys comin'?"

The other two got up. "Might as well," said one, "That's what we come for." They walked toward the large building.

"They know I'm not going," said Jody. "I guess they think you're not going either."

"You're really not?" asked Charlie.

"No. I never go anymore. Pam won't let me touch her for a month if she finds out. And with Red being here, she'll find out."

"You used to though?"

"Hell, yes. I was over here all the time. Matter of fact this is where I cracked my cherry."

Charlie suddenly took his glass of tequila and drank it in one gulp. He could not breathe for a moment, and when he spoke, it was in a high squeak. "Jesus Christ Almighty!" he said. "Goddamn!"

Jody laughed so hard he knocked his beer over. He called the waiter and when he could control his laughter he asked, "Are you nervous?"

"Scared. Not nervous."

"Don't sweat it. Listen. Tell her she's your first. She'll like that and probably help you. You better go now."

"I will," said Charlie. "I don't want to, but I will." He drank from his beer. "That's one hell of a place over there. Is it really full of whores?"

"It's full of whores, alright, but it isn't as big as it looks. There's a patio in the middle. The building has a long hallway that goes completely around with rooms on both sides. The broads will open their doors when they hear you coming. Keep saying 'no' until you find what you want even if you have to go completely around. You can go around again."

Now Charlie laughed. "Anything else I should know, Daddy?"

"Yeah. Stay in the center of that hallway until you decide, because they'll be grabbing for you."

"Honest? Grab—you mean *grab?*"

Jody was patient. "Yeah, *grab!* Especially this early when there's little or no business. Get too close and they'll grab you by the balls. They hurt, too."

Charlie stood up, grinned somehow, and walked steadily toward the stone walk. But the only steady thing about him was his appearance. He did not feel the drink even though it had almost choked him to death. He knew he moved forward on courage alone; he was taking a walk he was destined to take and could not postpone, and now, suddenly this act to come was the most important thing in his life and he suffered such a paroxysm of shaking that he almost went to his knees before he reached the door because he knew he would fail. But he did reach the door and held himself up against it for a moment, then opened it and entered. He looked down the long hallway and froze where he stood, wanting to walk back out but unable to move and his view, almost distorted, revealed an endless twin line of open doors, each with a woman in a flimsy wrap, each figure diminishing in size as his gaze moved farther away, and the walls of the hall through the periphery of his vision also came toward each other until they converged seemingly miles away to merge with two tiny figures at the end of nowhere. But as he felt the beginnings of an unknown panic, he was startled out of it by the first two women, one on either side of him, barely a few feet before him, beckoning, talking to him even though he was temporarily a mute and, whereas those down the line were doll-like, a part of a fantasy, these two were real and he knew that as he walked each pair in turn would become real and he was terrified.

Then he moved, without willing it, he moved, and was nearly halfway to the end before he heard a voice or really looked at a woman, and now, struggling to keep from breaking into a run, he thought how he would walk out the door at the other end of the hall and now he could hear them, suddenly audible as if a radio had suddenly come on at full volume and what they said was not pretty, their words were not an aphrodisiac as they were intended to be and he looked at them and they were not beautiful. And indeed they did reach out for him, some offering a variety of services, but oddly they did not leave their doorways. As long as he remained in the center of the hall, he was safe, and he found it difficult to keep to the center, like walking on a line. He saw negresses, tall and yellow, squat and black as night, Orientals, Europeans, white Americans, and, of course, Mexicans.

When he reached the end of the hall there was no door, but he knew there was not meant to be one, and he turned the corner, looking carefully now at every one, knowing that he could walk completely around and return to the bar but his still trembling body told him he would stop before he reached the next corner.

He saw her up ahead to the left, standing out because all the others before and after her were foreign and she stood waiting, heavy, strong-thighed through a pale green, short transparent wrap, red faced almost florid, incredible blond hair down to her waist, with a wide smile on her fat, young, Brunhilde face; and he did not wait for her to make her pitch but walked straight into her room having but a vague feeling that he did so because she was white and here was security of sorts and outside was the last time he saw her smile.

She closed the door and said, "Le' see."

He looked at her and reached for his wallet, but she slapped his hand and said, "No—prick, le' see prick!"

He realized she did not speak English and wondered how he had ended up with a foreigner after all, and then he thought, what the hell? No one had told him about having to show his dingus, and he had what even to him was a weird thought that she would throw him out if it were not large enough and as he unzipped his Levis he had no feeling in his groin and he knew it was the end for him right here, but she took his limp penis and squeezed it, milked it, and again he thought, what the hell! He had no recollection whatever of the yearly hygiene lectures in the school gymnasium and he had no time to begin to think this out because she had shed her flimsy wrap and now lay on her back, legs open, knees up, shapeless feet flat on the cheap coverlet. He moved toward her as she waved jerkily for him to hurry and as he stood by the bed he saw her massive breasts hang heavily on either side of her almost to the bed but what caught his fascination was her crotch and he could only stare. Huge, it seemed, grotesque, skin and hair of darker hue, the labia wrinkled and falling in folds, and she reached down with both hands and opened the thing with an almost delicate movement and now he saw the bright red flesh and he again had wild thoughts, none finished. So this was it, this was what it was all about ... he would talk to her for a while ... ugly fucken thing and guys died for it ... he would talk to her ... pay her and get the hell out, but he knew he could not talk to her, ask her how come she's a whore, hear the story of her life but she did not know his language and instead he quickly shed his clothes because of everything he knew, had ever known, this was the only truth, this he must do and goddamn it, he would do it because if he did not Charlie Morgan might as well not exist, and so he climbed between her legs instinctively grinding his pelvis against her flesh but she was impatient and pushed and stuffed until he was inside. He was inside a woman for the first time and did not really know it because it was like being in a tremendous void and now she attempted to make him move and he tried, but it slipped out, and now she was angry, "You no fok! You no fok!" she screamed at him and tried to push him off but he insisted and used his strength to push her down, and she matched his strength and he repeated, "Just give me a chance, Goddamn it, just give me a chance!" even as she said, "You no fok, you no fok!" then they were kneeling, facing each other on the bed, breathing deeply from their short struggle and he saw hatred in her eyes and did not know that she was angry not only because she had done a stupid thing by forgetting to take the money first, and had now lost a trick, but also because as young as he was, he was a man and at this moment, using her, the enemy, and he thought that even if she was only a whore she was a human and a woman, and she hated him because he was incapable and could not please her and neither would ever know that he was right, but even as he thought this, he reached for his trousers and gave her the two dollars, then offered her another two if she would only help him and again she rejected him— "Go. You no fok!"

As he dressed, he felt the tears come to his eyes, but controlled them until he half-stumbled out into the hall, and now real panic because he had a long way to go and he was not certain he could make it before he began to really bawl and he knew that he would cry because Charlie Morgan had just died in that room, for that had not been Brunhilde but one of the furies and now all women were such and through a mist he saw a form to the left, next door, and he moved toward her, looking at her face. *My fucken luck!* This one was Mexican, and he desperately needed someone to whom he could talk, he who had always been so shy

46

could talk up a storm if he could find someone who could speak his language but as he looked into her face he saw that he knew her, knew her particular sadness which was unmistakable in her almost unlined face and an equally unmistakable compassion. Somewhere in time past he knew her and did not question her as she took his arm and said, "Yo sé, yo sé," as he could only utter, "¡no puedo! ¡No puedo!"

She sat him on the bed and sank down beside him, held him while he cried silently, then slowly undressed him talking all the time in Spanish, telling him not to cry, to cry until he was done, and she told him she had a son about his age somewhere, who knows where, and then they were naked on the bed and she held him and touched him as his cries subsided still talking to him and finally she was atop him, rubbing him with her body, holding him tightly yet tenderly and now she rolled over and he found that he was big and she took his hand and guided him into her and though he was ready she made him feel huge by gradually working her legs until they were closed and straddled her still within and she did not have to teach him more.

He remembered the music in her words although he did not understand her language, and he remembered the pleasure of being carefree. He was surprised that he did not remember her body, only the odor of it. And he returned to her twice with Jody before he left for Texas; Jody laughed and teased him that he was hooked on screwing.

He returned a third time alone and she was gone. He sat at the bar with his tequila and beer, feeling alone once again. He asked the bartender:

"That girl Rosa who worked in there, know where she went?"

"They're all named Rosa, kid, or María del Carmen, María del Rosario or María del Refugio," the bartender said, not unkindly. "I don't know who she was."

Charlie tried to describe her and found he could not.

"We really never see any of them," continued the bartender. "This place is different from the joints in town. Hustling drinks or ass is not allowed. Men come here to drink and talk. Many of them are businessmen and conduct some of their business here. If they want to fuck they take a stroll over there, if they don't nobody bothers them. The women are not allowed to come in here."

"How about the boss? He should know."

"He might, but I don't think so. There's a hell of a lot of them in there and they come and go. The man or men who own them move them around. The boss here pays the supplier. It's like owning a store—

47

there's a distributor and everyone makes a profit." He refilled the glass of tequila and brought another beer.

A young man, very black, walked in and sat beside him. "Mind if I join you? No one else here and I hate to drink alone."

Charlie was not rude, though his words sounded surly. "Suit yourself," he said.

"I'm Aloysius," said the youth. "Some try to call me Al, but I insist on Aloysius. Guess I'm as perverse as my mother, who insisted on giving us ridiculous names. I once knew a girl called Florida Washington."

Charlie laughed in spite of himself. "I'm Charlie," he said.

"Well, drink up, Charlie, and I'll buy you one."

Charlie was on the verge of refusing, then said, "Thanks. Why not?"

"Nobody said 'why not' fella. Why are you so low?"

He was on his third tequila and beer. He had never drunk this much, and his lips were a little numb but more than that, he felt morose. "Christ! I feel that everything Charlie Morgan ever does or touches turns to shit!"

"You must be Charlie Morgan."

"Yeah, I'm Charlie Morgan. Biggest Goddamn loser around!" He went on then and told all that he knew about himself, but especially what had occurred in the past few weeks. He had another drink, and another, and he knew he was quite drunk. And in the end, Aloysius said:

"Looks to me like you live a normal life, man. Everybody has it tough—your brothers had it tougher than you."

"No they didn't. They did what they wanted to do and they died."

"That's just it," said Aloysius. "They're dead."

"And why am I? I'm as dead as they are."

"You're alive man! You're alive. More than that, you don't have a worry in the world, Charlie, because you're *white*!"

He returned to El Paso shortly after that day, but not before he got to Janey Blair. It had been good, but something, he sensed, had happened to him.

He was hooked, Jody had said in jest, but he had been right. And neither he nor Charlie suspected on what. It was something out of history that had reached out for him. He was following the pattern of the Spaniard who, in getting hot for the Mexican, created the mestizo and sealed his own doom. He did not know it yet, but he was hooked on Mexicans and, perhaps a more dangerous condition, he was hooked on whores.

FIVE

Looking down at the two figures on the floor, he said, "Mamá."

She held a sheet to her to cover her breasts as she sat up. "¿Ya disperaste, mi'jo?" she asked. She did not think that he might be affected by her being in bed with a man. "Mira, quiero que conozcas a este señor. Es norteamericano. Se llama Chale Morgan."

"Buenos días," he said.

"Buenos días," said Charlie Morgan.

Chale Morgan. It had happened very quickly that day. It began to happen when he first opened his eyes, it continued after the man left, when he and his mother were having their breakfast. A second man came. Ramón had seen him twice talk to his mother, but always outside the door, on the roof. Now the man pushed the door in, did not knock.

"Is it you, Armando?" she asked.

"Yes, it is I, Armando. I wish to speak with you."

"The boy..."

"He will know about you sooner or later. It will be better, easier, if he begins to learn now. Keep him here."

His manner frightened her. She did not know why he seemed angry, had but a vague idea that she had done a thing that was forbidden. "What do you want?" she asked.

He was serious, not angry, and spoke almost in a kindly manner. "You are not allowed to have a lover. An occasional interlude, perhaps yes, but nothing permanent."

She said, "We are going to marry."

He laughed. "Don't be dumb. Even if he meant it, we would not allow it. Our girls are free to marry only if they marry well. In a few years, if you learn and behave yourself, you can make a good connection, and you go with our congratulations."

She sensed hope. "He is an American and they are all rich. That is a good connection, no?"

"No," he said. He would have laughed again but he felt a sorrow for her. "I know many Americans, and they are not all rich. As a matter of fact, most Americans are not rich. Many are as poor as you. Listen to me. For your own good you must not continue with this one."

But she was not accepting this. "I must remove myself from this life. I am going to marry and live decently. Leave me be!"

"Listen, listen." Again he tried to reason with kindness. "This is not up to me. I would allow a little of this to go on—just long enough for you to discover for yourself that he does not intend to marry you. But there are others who decide these things, and I cannot blame them. A man in your life would interfere with your work."

"I love him," she said.

"Now that is even worse. A whore cannot afford the luxury of love unless she is at the top, or quite far on the way down. I've told you that." He thought for a moment. "Be good now. I will not report this, especially because it has to do with Chale Morgan."

She was surprised. "You know him."

"Yes, I know him. Everybody in this colonia knows him. How do you think I learned so quickly. He has tried this other times, and he has been warned."

"That was before I knew him."

"Yes, but he has been warned. I have a liking for Chale Morgan, and I would feel sorry if he should be hurt."

That same afternoon Charlie Morgan returned. He spoke to Ramón's mother for a few minutes, then they gathered up their belongings and carried them downstairs, down the main stairs that were for the residents, not down the spiral, rusted iron ladder hugging the outside of the building, reserved for the domestics who lived on the roof. The blue van with FLETES Y MUDANZAS painted on it was always across the street and was now double-parked in front. They placed their things in the back, then pushed Ramón in and closed the doors. Chale Morgan and his mother rode in front with the driver. It was dark inside, but after a bit Ramón could see a desk, some chairs and lamps, a table and many boxes filled with books.

Now they were in Narvarte, in a beautiful neighborhood, and not on a roof. But three days later the driver of the van came.

"Chale, mano," he said. "Fíjate que les dije que te traje aquí."

"Pendejo! Baboso!" Charlie Morgan was very red in the face. But the harm was done.

This time they moved across to the northern part of the city, to Estrella, and they were there a week before Charlie came running in, a look of both anger and fright on his face. By now his few pieces of furniture and his books had been left behind. They traveled only with what they could carry. And it was obvious that he had little money. They went to the southernmost part of the district now, on the road to Xochimilco, on the fringe of the Pedregal. Here they lived in a man-made cave, built with huge lava rocks, and were safe there for a time.

Chale Morgan was drinking now, and where he got the money Ramón did not know, for they had barely enough to eat. For a time his mother had been sullen and quiet, and then one night he was wakened by loud noises and arguing and he saw Chale Morgan strike his mother on the face. Ramón did not cry; he feigned sleep, and she was not aware he knew.

Now he was many times awake when they thought him asleep. And Chale Morgan would come in at midnight or in the early morning hours to call his mother, and she would leave with him for an hour or two. Sometimes this happened two or three times a night, and the next day Chale would have drinking alcohol. He was now down to the lowest drink in Mexico, mixing it with epasote. He would become sentimental, would talk to Ramón who shivered from the dampness of the cave now in the rainy season.

"Be a good soldier," he would say, then in Spanish would assure him that soon they would go away to the far north. Everything would be different.

Be a good soldier! He did not know what that phrase meant, but he never forgot the words.

SIX

Clemente Chacón drove into his allotted space in the parking lot of the First Bank of the Southwest. It was the newest building in the city. The Company had a full half of a floor, a foreign consulate had the other half. As he walked toward the entrance to the building he could not remember having parked his car, yet he could still see the bold letters MR. CHACON on the gutter to his slot. He went toward the rear, to the private elevator which opened to a foyer leading to his and Mr. Smith's offices.

He smiled to himself. Queli wanted him to change his name. To what—Smith? It seemed that most insurance executives were named Smith. He went into his office and opened another door leading into the bullpen. Small offices of supervisors and Payroll lined the walls. In the center, salesmen and clerical workers had desks. Theirs was a fully autonomous operation. Every record in their district was here; the home office had it on microfilm. He took his coat off as he watched the staff moving in. He closed the door and turned to see Miss Gray, his secretary, come in with his coffee. He noticed she did not bring hers this morning—they had made it a practice to spend the first fifteen minutes of the day over coffee, discussing the day's schedule.

"Good morning, Clem," she said. "The young men are here."

"The young men?"

"The boys from the University—from MACHOS—remember, the Militant Arm of the Chicano Organization for Students."

"Oh, those boys." He had completely forgot that in a weak moment he had allowed himself to be scheduled for today. He had tried to put it off for a week or two, although he was always willing to talk to representatives of the Chicano community, but they had been insistent that they must see him now. "Alright, send them in."

There were three of them. As they walked in they shook his hand, "Good morning, Mr. Chacón. Good of you to see us at this hour. We know what a busy day this will be for you." They gave him the Chicano handshake, which always made him uncomfortable, as if he were playing a grade school game. The first time someone had handled his hand like that he had the suspicion that the fellow was attempting to tickle his palm.

"It's always good to see you boys," he said. "Sit down. What can I do for you?"

Two of them took chairs. The third stood alongside the others, arms folded. He was very dark, very Indian, and he stared at Clemente with a look that could only be described as inscrutable, yet somehow hostile.

The speaker had a thin mustache and a slender, hatchet-like face. He held a notebook open, as if to take notes. "My name is Cipriano Cantú," he said. Clemente did not catch the names of the other two. "We come for your help, Mr. Chacón. As a rule, we do not disturb our Chicanos who are making it in the white man's world. Those of you who do this are very valuable to the movement. You serve as an example of what our young people can aspire to, you have shown that you can compete alongside the Anglo in an Anglo endeavor. Many of you, of course, are really vendidos, hold jobs like Niggers-in-Residence, and really don't give a shit for our people. We know that you have been different. We know about you. You contribute money to our cause—deductible, or it may come from your firm, but at least you don't give it to the SPCA. You have also joined LULAC and La Raza Unida even though you never appear at any of our functions. I have also seen you occasionally helping out at the Boys' Club. We know you don't have to do those things. Therefore you must be with us."

Clemente felt a constriction in his stomach. This young man was too certain, too sure of what he would ask, and it did not seem that he would accept denial. "I have done what I could. Obviously, I could not become overtly active or I wouldn't be where I am today. I feel for my people. I was born in the Chamizal in El Paso, before it was returned. Now I wonder if that means I'm really a Mexican citizen. I grew up in the streets of the city. I have known hunger, I have been a thief, a pimp, and survived in the war of the streets we know so well. Somehow I never got involved in drugs, but I was tempted. So why should I not help my people in my way?" He must stop this—he was talking much too much. *Tell them nothing,* Mario had said, and here he was telling these young men that he was frightened. He must control his fright, but he could not because he did not know why he was afraid. And why even mention the idea of nationality?

"We know all that. We know a little more. But now the time has come for you to begin to sacrifice a bit. You have given money because you can afford it and, I repeat, some is Company good-will money. Now in the name of the Movement, in the name of MACHOS, we are asking you to come out in the open. We are facing several crises. We are lining up Chicanos who are solid American citizens. Successful people in the business world, in the judiciary, in the dirty business of running this city in the interest of whitey. We must have and must show unity when we present our demands."

"Demands?"

"Demands! We have scheduled a press conference for tomorrow. As you know, the Raza Unida is holding its first national convention in El Paso beginning tonight. Some members have been invited to your success ritual tonight also. And last night one of our delegates was shot and killed by a white racist. Tomorrow our Chicano businessmen, our judges, Justices of the Peace, any one of our people who has elevated himself above that low level reserved for us will speak out against that brutal murder. Up until now we believed that you had gone as far as you could go in your business. We were really surprised that they would go so far as to promote you to the position you will receive today. It means that they are really frightened, to give you such a responsibility, unless you are to be a mere figurehead."

Clemente was now angry. That fear of a moment ago was forgotten. "What the hell do you mean 'figurehead'?" He clenched and unclenched his fists, not wanting to remember the long days and nights, the sacrifices, the entire business of his dissatisfaction with his marriage—this which must be discussed and corrected soon—and he calmed himself to say, "When you say this, you are saying that we Mexicans don't have the intellectual capacity, the drive, the industry necessary to meet people of another culture, another blood, on their terms. Do you mean this? If you do, then we *are* in trouble, because then we don't stand a chance."

The young man actually blushed. "No," he said. "I do not mean that. I mean that the white man will not let us get ahead. We are capable, but he will stifle us, he will keep us down as he has always done. And when he does allow us to better ourselves it is strictly PR bullshit. He is buying you and he is buying me, simply because I'll buy his fucken insurance because he has moved you up the ladder. He is not being democratic. It is simply good business."

"There is where you and I differ," said Clemente, and he was aware that he was in a contest, but in a contest where his opponent did not hear him. "It is also good business to reward someone for doing a good job, to promote someone for his ability and performance. I sold one million dollars' worth of business this past year, not counting what my people did on the debit end. I am being promoted and given a pay raise because of that. I would not accept this if it were based simply on the fact that I am Mexican."

There was almost a minute of silence. The young man scribbled on his pad. Then he looked up. "Hay otra cosa de que tenemos que hablar." When Clemente did not answer, he continued, "We will have a confrontation with the administration of the University on Monday. We did it in Colorado a couple of years ago—we are doing it all over the country and we should have done it here by now."

Clemente now also spoke in Spanish. "Y eso de la universidad, ¿qué? Yo no sé nada de la universidad."

"I am going to tell you about the University."

The other man who was seated now spoke. "Forty percent or more of the student body of the Univeristy are Chicano. We have good representation on the faculty—28 professors, I think, but there has been no progress in securing administrative positions for our people."

The second young man spoke again. "On Monday we will face the President of the University. We have something to work on—there is a new opening, Director of Development. They are planning to place an Army man—thirty years' service, a Brigadier, in this position. They are not even considering a Chicano!"

Clemente placed his head in his hands. He rubbed his eyes, and said, "Jesus, this is unreal. You really don't know anything, do you? Development means raising money for the University. If this Brigadier didn't make it higher than he has in thirty years, he isn't much good, but he can be good for this job. Realistically, if he brings a million dollars into the University, you will get a certain percentage, perhaps get a few more Mexican kids in school. This fellow, and we can assume that he has a history of incompetency, will talk to old, Anglo, rich people, he will sip tea with them, and he will remind them that Texas is a big state. They will like that, and he will then tell them that because it is so big, there is one University that is not getting enough money because it is removed, out of the way. He won't say that forty percent of the student body is made up of poor Mexican-Americans who need a break, because then he will get nothing. He will talk about the poor white folks' youngsters who need a place to study. What would you do? Have someone like Cuauhtémoc over there do the fund-raising?" He waved toward the third youth, stolid, arms still crossed. "This army soldier will sip his tea, maybe attend Sunday morning services, talk to the neighbors and will come home with a good portion of his host's Santa Gertrudis cattle or an oil well or two. They will all kneel and pray to Christ—thank the Lord

55

that He has given them the wherewithal to help provide an education for their own. They are opinionated people, they are WASPS and most of them are bigoted. So why not have a bigot go after their money?"

"Because that must change."

"Because that must change you get no money."

"A Chicano professor at the University, a scholar, has placed his job on the line on this issue. He has applied for the position and will resign if he is turned down."

Clemente's business sense was much too good to accept this. "He does not have another job if the administration turns him down?" he asked. "Does the University think he is too valuable to lose? You know right now Chicano and nigger professors are big on the market. Every university and college in the country wants at least one of them and would prefer one of each. Makes for good relations with HEW."

"He has offers. And moneywise he can do better. Also, in terms of status, one of the offers will make gains for us."

Clemente laughed. "Then he is not putting his job on the line, as you say. And his new position may very well be that position of tokenism you have accused me of."

The young man closed his notebook. He looked up, ferret-like, but his companion anticipated him and spoke. "We did not come here to discuss your views, which obviously are not in line with ours. We want to know if you will join us tomorrow for the press conference?"

"I cannot help you because tomorrow I fly to Boston to meet with the Board of my Company. That could also make gains for you, I suppose, a Chicanito flying to New England to confer with the owners and leaders of one of the great insurance companies in America. You won't believe me, but I must tell you that essentially I believe in what you do. I don't believe in your tactics but I admire your total commitment in the interest of removing inequities. No, I cannot be with you tomorrow, but I am more honest than your scholar. I spoke of gains, using your term, but I am not thinking of gains for my people, I am thinking of myself and my family. I will also tell you that I would not go with you in any case. I cannot go before the press to talk about something I know nothing about. The killing—I do not know the victim, I do not know the killer. I know nothing of the incident."

The sharp-faced one spoke, "But he was a Chicano, and I am telling you he was killed by a racist. Can you not take my word?"

"You are also a racist, so I cannot."

The young man had opened his pad again. Now he closed it and stood up. He said, "Denle sus chingazos."

The silent one unfolded his arms and moved. Clemente was filled with anger and frustration. He had no fear now and rose to defend himself, but the other was very quick. He felt the first blow strongly below the solar plexus; he did not feel the blows that followed, although he was conscious. He was aware that he was on the floor. He tried to raise his arms to protect his head, but he could not move them. The second young man was over him now and kicked him in the ribs. He did not see the leader, did not hear him say, "Vámonos ya," and he was alone.

The paralysis did not last long. He remembered vaguely that the boy had said something as he was being beaten. Something important. It came to him suddenly, *"I said we know about you. We even know about Chale Morgan."*

Now he had something to fear.

Miss Gray and Mr. Smith's secretary came in. Mrs. Knickrem, Ruth, was not pretty, but she was handsome despite an overly large nose that was almost bulbous. Her rimless glasses, the small chain that attached them to her head, gave her the look of a matron, or a fifty year-old spinster. She was, in fact, fiftyish and a matron. Pregnant at age eighteen, she had been widowed by a sniper's bullet in Okinawa. For many years she hated Japs—not a specific Japanese, only Japs—and now she had transferred that hate to wars. She hated war. Now, after her husband's death, she used her widow's benefits to go to a good business school. Her son, who was now making himself a name in Florida real estate, and who was forever after her to retire there, had got himself through college on the basis that he was the orphaned son of a serviceman killed in action. She had not remarried.

But whereas her face and her manner implied respectability, her body did not. Obviously she took care of herself. And Clemente lay on the floor looking up her skirt. They were talking to him, but he could not make sense of their words. He looked at Ruth Knickrem's fine legs and on up under her short skirt. She wore only panty hose, and the flesh of her thighs and buttocks looked firm and young. Despite his pain, he felt uncontrollably, suddenly, the filling of his crotch. He wanted to reach up and pull her down to him, to bury himself within her, in fact he did extend an arm, which she took to help him up. But he let go her hand because there was a suffering he wanted eased, not help to get off the floor.

He stood up on his own and saw Mr. Smith standing alongside Mrs. Knickrem. Small and dapper, always immaculately groomed, Virgil Smith looked like someone's retired grandfather on his way to walk the dog for his daily pee. Seeing the two, looking like man and wife, Clemente knew. As if he had seen them in coitus, he knew.

"Jesus Christ, Clem! What in hell is going on here?" Virgil Smith spoke in a surprisingly strong voice.

"I had a visit from my 'people'."

"Well, Goddammit, what did you do to have them knock you about like that?"

"Nothing. Because I do nothing I am a vendido—an Uncle Tom, a Tío Taco, in short, a sellout." In his mind, *Charlie Morgan—Chale.*

Miss Gray handed Clemente a water glass half-filled with brandy. "This is medicine," she said, anticipating his refusal. "Take it like a good soldier."

Like a good soldier! Good old Charlie Morgan! How much did they know about him?

Virgil Smith said, "Ruth, get that industrial quack up here to doctor Clem up. Then call the police. Don't talk to any fucken sergeant—get the Chief if you have to pull the son of a bitch off the saddle." Mr. Smith was given to obscenities under stress, and coming from him the words did sound obscene. "Son of a bitch! Come in here as pretty as you please and kick the shit out of my best man! What is it you didn't or won't do?"

"They want me to be more militant—to speak up in the interest of the Chicano, that sort of thing. And what worth would I be to the Company or to them if I did that? I told them the truth. I refused."

"Good for you," said Virgil Smith. "Son of a bitch!"

"The doctor will be right up," said Ruth.

"Call him back. Tell him not to come. And don't call the police," said Clemente.

"Don't call the cops?" Virgil Smith was excited. "We can't allow this kind of horseshit to go on!"

"Be sensible, Virgil," said Clemente. "You don't want to publicize this. Bad for our image, bad for your sales. It won't happen again. Those young men and I know exactly where we stand. After all, I *am* one of them. They will wonder for a short time whether they will be hit. I am a Mexican and I have friends. These lads know that all it would take is a phone call. Down deep, though, they know I will not do it. If I should, they would make it so miserable for the Company that I would be removed. You know our paternalistic relationship with the Mexican-American and Negro community. You know our sales pick up every time we pay for the burial of a child who has died of malnutrition or sometimes, even, of parental neglect. Then again, these punks will keep quiet because they really want me to succeed. They will hate me, ignore me or curse me, but they will do nothing to have the 'white' man destroy me. You will notice they did not touch my face. Why? Because they will not spoil my day. They have a strange idea about la familia. The familia concept insists that we keep our things to ourselves. Our enemy, the 'white' man, will never have our support against one of us. So I'm home free. I suppose it was good that this happened now. I will not be disturbed again." As he said these words he knew he should not worry about the reference to Charlie Morgan. Yet, he retained a slight apprehension. Why had they mentioned Charlie?

"I hope you know what you are doing," said Virgil Smith. "I'd have the murdering bastards behind bars." He was still indignant as he continued. "Christ, I've been along this border for many years, and I swear I don't really know you people."

"Don't try," said Clemente. As they walked out, he watched the flowing motion of Ruth Knickrem's back and buttocks.

He sat with his head in his hands. He heard the door close. And then Lucinda Gray was somehow perched on one arm of his chair. She reached around and took his head. With her other arm she pulled him to her breast. He was very much aware of her body as she said:

"I'm so sorry, Clem. I'm so sorry."

He allowed her to turn his face toward her own. He saw tears stream down her cheeks, and then tasted them as she brought her mouth down to his, felt her lips soft, her tongue in his mouth.

They stood up and he walked, deeply affected, across the carpeted floor.

She asked, "Are you hurt? Are you certain you're alright?"

"I'm fine," he said. And despite his aches and pains, he really was. He seemed surprised at that. "You know," he said. "I can't explain what I feel. Relief, I guess. I suppose I have been waiting for some demand. I'm glad it wasn't something more important. They could have really hurt me."

"Or killed you," she said. She started to reach out a hand, but knew that he would not let her touch him now.

"Give me a few minutes to pull myself together, OK? Then tell Mr. Smith I would like a minute with him before he goes out."

He took his shirt and tie off and went into his bathroom where he washed his face and then thoroughly rinsed it with cold water. He went out for his shirt and tie, and while dressing noticed a small rent in his shirt. For a moment he thought of having someone go out and buy another one, then he thought, the hell with it. He would go home and change later. He felt his groin under his pants—this was a banner day, three times now he had felt almost uncontrollably horny. He thought warmly, pleasantly, and with more than a little regret, of Lucinda Gray.

They had not discussed the kiss, had made no mention of it, and it had been the only time this had happened. He knew Lucinda was too good a secretary to allow it to happen again. But whereas Mrs. Knickrem had a ripe, full, sexy body and wore short skirts, Lucinda had it all. She was beautiful, intelligent and young. Also, she seemed to never be completely dressed. Barely twenty-one, she had come to him at age nineteen, and he interviewed her because he could not be rude. He had been ready to reject her out of hand.

But there had been something determined about her, despite a wistful look as she talked which was a detriment to her while being interviewed for a job. She told him her story; in fact, she told him more than he wanted to hear.

She had had an abortion at age fifteen, and this was immediately distasteful to him. Yet, she graduated from high school while still sixteen. A few months later, she had married her second lieutenant, father of her never-born child, at Fort Carson. Both were army brats, both sets of parents stationed in Colorado. Their earlier indiscretion was forgotten. When she was seventeen, they were in West Germany, she deliriously happy until she discovered that her tall, husky, beautiful husband was double-gaited. It was not a bad scene until he called in his lover, young, whipcord straight Captain Young. Captain Young's solution was simple—a ménage à trois—and now the entire thing became ugly because she reacted so strongly. Not only did she object; hell, she could not even pronounce it.

So she left. She did not want to arrive without being able to think things out. She wanted time, and when the Army insisted that she fly, she paid her own way on a boat.

"Mr. Chacón," she had said. "I had a chance to think on that voyage. The first thing I learned was that I was alone. I could not go home. My father was in Viet Nam competing with my father-in-law for his first star; my mother was in Colorado Springs helping him get it. Of course my mother-in-law was also there helping her husband. Actually, she is no longer my mother-in-law. I stopped in New York for a few days and went to the New York City Library. I had seen, in all my travels, that women could always find work if they could type a letter, so I looked for a good business school. I also paid twenty-five dollars to a testing outfit. They told me I had an IQ of 137 and should be a computer programmer. For the next few decades this would be the greatest field. They gave me a list of schools—universities—to consider. They did not consider I might not like computer programming. I *knew* I didn't, so I looked for a good business school.

"I found one across the river in Newark—an uglier city you will never find—but it was a good school—Berkeley Business School, and I was there a year. My husband paid for everything. He was afraid that I would tell my family why I had left him. It did not occur to him that I did not go home because if my father should know, his sense of duty would be so great that Bobby, my husband, and Reggie, Captain Young, would be out of the Army along with their friends of mutual inclinations. I was there a year, and since my father was now in North Carolina with his first star, my mother went there and I went to Colorado Springs. I had the idea I had to go to the place where I married to get an annulment. So I became a Kelly Girl, got the annulment quietly, regained my maiden name, which wasn't much because Bobby's name is Black, so I went from Mrs. Black to Miss Gray. I came here because the only times I remember as really happy times were when my father was stationed at Bliss."

Clemente stood up and walked to the door. He saw perhaps fifteen young women standing or sitting in the anteroom. He did not speak and Lucinda Gray continued. "I am a competent secretary. I cannot help that I look as I do. I thought of wearing something severe for this interview, but decided that would make me a phoney. I want to know now. I don't want to wait through the afternoon or until tomorrow to know. Tell me now, so that I can look elsewhere."

Clemente motioned to Mrs. Knickrem. She came in, not showing her feelings in any way, with a purposely composed face.

"Send them away. When they're gone..."

She looked at Lucinda Gray, legs crossed, a beaded purse on her thigh, a wisp of a bead-like skirt far up on her leg, and she interrupted: "Is that wise, Mr. Chacón?"

He looked up and she recognized her error. "I'm sorry," and she was nervous, but she said, "Some of them have been here all morning. I thought you would like to hear my thoughts on each applicant..."

"If you wish to waste more of their time, fine. Keep them here all afternoon. But I want Miss Gray completely oriented before tomorrow. I want you to take her in and introduce her to the staff."

"Very well, Mr. Chacón." Mrs. Knickrem walked out with immense dignity.

"Well, Miss Gray," said Clemente. "I'm pleased to have you with us. As they say in the business, welcome aboard. Are there any questions? I don't talk salary or things like that. Mrs. Knickrem will take you to the accountant and she will tell you everything you need to know for the present."

"One or two questions, Mr. Chacón. Do you always make your decisions in this way?"

"You asked for a quick decision, no? But, yes, I usually do."

"One more thing. Do you feel there may be more than just a job to this? I don't want you to be deceived."

He began to laugh, then stopped because she was so serious. "You are a lovely young woman. I will be happy to see you here. But that is all—I feel you can be an asset to our operation. You have nothing to fear."

She was embarrassed, contrite. "You must understand, I want so much to make good on my ability."

"I want that too," he said. "And I know you will."

SEVEN

Virgil Smith looked up from his desk as Clemente entered his office. "Be with you in a minute," he said. "Have to sign a few more things."

Clemente looked at the older man with respect, admiration and a sense of gratitude. This man had somehow made it possible, had hired him, in fact, had watched his progress, had promoted him from those early terrible days on the sidewalks selling debit insurance to poor Mexicans and poorer Negroes, if this last was possible. Three years later he had progressed to a desk, overseeing a staff of other men, some who had been there when he came, who pounded the pavement daily, selling and collecting twenty-five cents a week policies. Two years of this, with visible growth to the Company, and he became head of all departments in the city. Virgil Smith had moved up accordingly and was now in charge of the entire state. Again they were moving up together, but with the reorganization of the entire Company, Clemente would head four states when he took Virgil's job tonight, and it was no longer only debit; he had sold one million dollars of insurance to industry this past year. Mr. Smith would now have all the western states.

Virgil Smith walked around from his desk. He was genuinely concerned as he put out a hand, and asked, "Are you alright, boy? It's not too late to get those bastards!"

"I'm okay. I can forget it," said Clemente. "Let's all forget it."

"OK, if you want it that way," said Virgil Smith. "But Christ!" His small body trembled with indignation. He had sincere affection for this young man. He recognized his abilities, had nurtured and encouraged his aspirations. They had always dealt honestly with each other—and the fact that he had a hard-on for the younger man's wife did not bother him. That was outside of business. Even his own wife knew that Virgil Smith was the type of man who must have strange stuff now and then. He did not think about this, as he did not think about the fact that sooner or later he would have the lovely Queli. Had he known how really Mexican Clemente was, how such an act could destroy him, perhaps destroy Virgil also, he would have been appalled. This was simply not important.

"I got to thinking this morning," Clemente was saying, "that the Company could get very good national copy out of this if handled right."

Virgil laughed as if he had put one over on him. "I been way ahead of you, boy. Calhoun should be here any minute now; press conference tonight before the event. News coverage, film clips, everything. *Time, Life, Wall Street Journal, National Observer, Christian Science Monitor,* even some guy from Mexico City, *El Universal.* Kinda funny for you to be featured in Mexico City," he punched Clemente on the arm, "Lovely city and you haven't ever been there!" He walked around, rubbed his hands and returned to Clemente. "When we get moving again, take a break. Take that stunning wife of yours and spend a couple of weeks there. Kinda hard on your screwing cause it's so high up, you know—but shit, it doesn't seem to bother the natives. Fucken kids all over the place!"

Clemente laughed. Virgil Smith always ended up with this.

"Acapulco may be better," said Mr. Smith. "Sea level, you know." Then he turned again, and because they were this way together, he sounded triumphant. "How come I had to come up with it? You embarrassed about arranging your own publicity?"

"Maybe," said Clemente. "I thought about why it slipped my mind. It could have been that I haven't accepted the position yet."

"Well, Jesus Christ on a Polack crutch!" Virgil Smith was furious. "What the hell is all this for? Anyway, who arranged the other interviews?"

It was true. He had arranged for Clemente to see three people—all good opportunities—because he was certain of Clemente's judgment. He believed that it was better for Clemente to remain with him.

Clemente laughed again. "OK, you did all those things and I refused every offer, didn't I. But I have one more—across the border. In fact, I will have lunch with them today. These people are from the interior; one of them flew out from Mexico City. They think I can't refuse what they have to offer."

"Jesus Christ! Why haven't I been told?"

"Because I can't accept their offer. We plan to buy a small insurance company in Mexico. Operating along the lines of what we do, it has the potential for growth. I'm prepared to invest in the company but the Mexicans want my expertise. Full-time. I will consult, but I will not live in Mexico."

Virgil Smith breathed hard. "Oh, I worked too hard, almost placed my job on the line, you understand, to get you this deal. Don't fuck me up."

"Don't worry," said Clemente. "I am an American, remember?"

Virgil Smith moved to his telephone. "That cocksucker—I never have liked the son of a bitch—makes one wait on him. If I ever become president of this Company—I can, you know—I'm getting rid of that prick!"

Clemente did not comment. He knew Max Calhoun, the PR man. And he agreed with his boss.

"Ruth," Virgil Smith said, "if that son of a bitch is not here in five minutes, get me Mr. Smith in Hartford."

The voice came back almost immediately, static, "Mr. Calhoun is coming in the door right now. Shall I send him right in?"

"Now, what the hell do you think, Ruth?"

Max Calhoun came in. Huge, expansive, a stereotype. "Virgil, Clem, it's been some time."

Virgil Smith did not conceal his displeasure. "Don't give me that sweet horseshit! This is a busy day. What've you lined up?"

Max Calhoun gave him a long look. "They're all here," he said. "Just waiting for my call."

"Well, call them," said Virgil Smith.

"I thought I should have a chat with Clem first. Sort of get him ready," said the PR man.

"Get him ready?" Virgil almost squealed in his anger. "For what?"

Calhoun remained calm. "Look," he said. "I know my line of work, you know yours. I've already briefed the media. In a few days Clem will be a household word—in a month no one will remember his name, but they will remember the Company. Watch your curve climb, Virg!"

Virgil Smith understood this, and he now said, "OK, make your call. You got an hour."

"What do you want, Max?" asked Clemente.

"Give them plenty of facts on your early life. Lay it on. Show how hard you fought on the way up and how the Company, through Virg here, helped you succeed. We'll send a photo crew to take pictures of your barrio."

"Shall I tell them I was a pimp at age ten?"

"Jesus Christ, no!" said Calhoun. He looked at Clemente, not believing him. "That isn't true anyway, is it?"

Virgil smoothly said, "God's honest truth," and exhaled smoke coolly through his nostrils.

Calhoun still doubted, but he said, "OK. Make up things but none of that kind of crap. We must get across the idea that you had a miserable life, but through hard work and the equal opportunity offered by the Company you have achieved success."

Clemente grinned. "I don't have to make up a damn thing. I have had a shitty time of it."

"Keep to that story," said Calhoun. "And tonight when you speak at the banquet, it will be like an acceptance speech, although we know you are already promoted. The ceremonies will be video-taped, and I want you to use that accent you used to affect."

"It was real," said Clemente, "and I will not use it."

"The hell you won't," said Calhoun. "You've got to use it."

Clemente said, coldly, "I don't have to do a fucken thing."

Calhoun turned to Smith. "Tell him, Virg, for Chrissakes! That's an important part of the entire package."

"You heard him," said Virgil calmly. "He doesn't have to do a fucken thing."

"He'll do it if you order him to do it."

"No, he won't. Also I would never ask him to do it. I happen to know how hard he worked to rid himself of it. And anyway, are you trying to get across the idea that the Company is so democratic that we promote semi-literates? You push that too far and the idea you will publicize is that this promotion is tokenism. I will not have that. Clem got this job on his performance, Company loyalty, and most important because he is the best man for the position."

Now it was Calhoun's turn to understand. "I guess you're right at that," he said. "But Clem is going to surprise hell out of the press. I told them he had one hell of an accent."

Clemente laughed. "Sheet," he said. The other two laughed also. Calhoun asked:

"How much do you know about your new job?"

"Everything."

"They will ask you. Do you have certain plans, moves you will make?"

"I'll outline them—if only briefly—in the speech tonight," answered Clemente.

"Anything I should know now?"

Clemente now stood up. "Yes, one thing. I'm going to hire my own Public Relations man."

"Fine idea," said Calhoun. "I have just the man for you. How soon do you want him?"

"You chose not to hear me," said Clemente. "I said *my own* PR man. Not someone who answers to you."

Virgil Smith said, "I didn't know that. Why didn't you tell me?"

"Because you didn't ask me. And because I will have the authority to make such decisions." Virgil said no more.

Calhoun, however, was now angry. "You can't do that, Clem. You know the Company rule is to fill these jobs from within!"

"I know corporate policy as well as you do. We go outside when we don't have the capability within the Company. Send your men to me, one by one, or collectively. I'll interview them, and if I find my man, I'll put him to work. But I won't find him because there is one qualification that will be lacking."

"Try me," said Calhoun.

"How many Mexicans on your staff, Max?"

Virgil could not remain silent now. "Goddamn, Clem. What are you doing?"

Clemente struggled to not be angry. "Are you also going to tell me that a Mexican is not capable of doing the job?"

Calhoun interrupted and turned to Virgil. "Can't you see? Some of the solid people in the Company were afraid of just this. He's bringing his family in—giving lush jobs to any relative who can read and write!"

Virgil was white in his anger. He stood up and walked to Calhoun and said, "Don't you ever again say anything like that in my presence or one of us will surely leave the Company, and I assure you it will not be me."

Clemente faced the window, looked down below toward the parking lot, saw his small foreign-like car and visualized his name at the parking space. He said in a kind voice, "I didn't bring it up, Virgil, because I knew you would agree to it. We have been together for a long time. I know how you think. I simply don't think a half-assed New Englander can perform in border states." He pressed a button on the intercom. "Miss Gray, please bring in the PR folder."

Virgil Smith took it. Calhoun said, "I'd like to see that."

Clemente said flatly, "You can't."

Virgil glanced through it quickly. "Sorry, boy," he said to Clemente. "You're right, of course. Damn fine job . . . we'll go over it together to see if you slipped up somewhere. But we really must tell this son of a bitch some of it. He's not completely stupid, just slow." He walked again toward Calhoun and spoke in his business voice. "You see, Max, Clem will hire a Mexican PR man for the same reason I had him promoted. I know that Clem can do a fine, first-rate job in any one of our districts, but he will do a great job here. Why? Not because as a Mexican the Chicanos will be attracted to do business with him, but because he knows them, knows the Mexican mystique, the Mexican mind. We have a singular problem out here, and he knows it. In the Southwest, a great deal of our business is with the Spanish surnamed. We are in business to make money—we provide a service for it, and we use that money to make more money. You told me you knew your job; well, Clem is an expert at his also. I know that or I would have never pushed so hard to get him. He has some very good offers, you know." He waved the folder in his small fist. "He will get his PR man, don't even enjoy a small doubt. It's all here in this package, and believe me this boy does his homework."

But Calhoun was not convinced. "I don't think so," he said. "They'll never agree to such nonsense and, of course, in this I will be consulted. You know what my recommendation will be."

"Of course you will be consulted," said Virgil Smith, and now he smiled. "And of course I know what you will recommend. So I will save you the trouble of having to make a recommendation based on your half-assed petty prejudices. Christ, you're not even honest enough to have big prejudices. I told you the Company is in business to make money and I will keep you from obstructing this goal."

He turned to Clemente who was again at the window, his back toward them. "You have the go-ahead, Clem. Hire your man." He turned to Calhoun and continued in his mild yet resonant voice, "Now Max, you understand that you will not be consulted as to whether Virgil Smith has made a right decision."

Max Calhoun walked out of the room.

Clemente turned. He had no real feeling about what had transpired. He knew his superior's business mind. He had worked hard and long on this project, anticipating Virgil's every question, and had confidence in his justifications.

He said, "I have a man in mind. I must see if I can find him today. He's hungry and may have taken something else."

"I'll study this a while," said Virgil. "A couple of the big boys will be here tonight and I must have a plan of attack."

Clemente now allowed himself a smile. In the foyer, walking toward Miss Gray's desk he grew pensive. "I gave you a name and address some time ago. Man named Villegas."

"I have it," she said, pulling a file card. "Natividad Villegas, address, no information."

"I have all I need," he said. "Get a boy to run out and find him and bring him back in a cab. Tell him that I have a job for him and want him here in half an hour to discuss it. I don't want to be bothered by anyone for about fifteen minutes. Not even by Mr. Smith."

EIGHT

He closed the door to his office and stood for a moment leaning against it. He was not tired, but his body was extremely sore, suddenly more painful than during the actual beating. He was dizzy, breathed deeply, then moved to his desk. He took his key ring and opened the deep bottom drawer and removed an expensive leather case which he opened with another key. He took an old, cheap tape recorder from the case and placed it on the desk. He leaned back and closed his eyes for a moment, then reached forward and turned the switch.

"Hey, meestair! You wanna fok my seestair?" There were garbled sounds, the noise of honking automobiles, then:

"She virgin, meestair. Thirteen years old, verry clean!"

Again he sat with Mario near the bridge. Again looking across at the buildings a few short blocks distant, but worlds away. Suddenly, Mario jumped up.

"A chingao," he said. "Ay vienen unos mayates. ¡Jijo, cómo me gusta platicar con mayates!"

Ramón did not know what a mayate was, looked up to see a group of Negro soldiers walking toward them. As they came near, Mario spoke out:

"Hey mans! Lookeeng for leetle poosey?"

They stopped together, as if in review, and looked at him speechless.

"Or," Mario continued, "maybe you want beeg poosey." He laughed at his own joke, and suddenly one of the young black men leaned forward and began to laugh.

Mario laughed back with all his soul and said to Ramón, "¡Pero mira qué bonitos dientes tiene este cabrón!"

The black youth was waving his friends back. "Come lissen to this little dude." They gathered around the two little boys, and Mario, still smiling looked them over, selected his pigeon, and spoke directly to him, "Wanna fuck, mother fucker?"

The soldier looked at him for a moment as if in shock, very seriously, then burst into a paroxysm of laughter. He spun around, not unlike a whirling dervish, and his companions took hold of his arms, but his laughter was infectious and now everyone including Ramón and Mario was laughing, and the youth said suddenly, placing his face very near Mario's, leaning down from a great height, "Yew know what you talking about, boy?"

Mario did not answer. Instead he said, "I been fucking since I had seven years; she had forty, but I love her because it was my first woman." The soldiers did not quite disbelieve him because he spoke to them so seriously. He continued to speak directly to one of them. "But mebbe you one a' those who don' like women—OK, get you boy. Mebbe you want shooting gallery. Got taxi down the street—driver deaf and dumb. Take you to dreamland—anything you want Mario get."

The soldier said, "Sh-e-e-e-t, man. Too early for that stuff. We jes' got here. Ain't seen nothin' yet."

Mario imitated him perfectly. "Sh-e-e-e-t, man," he said. "You strong boy. Do it now, see the sights of Old Mexico, then do it again before you go back to the base. A double header jes' like the Blookin Dodgers—Jackie Robinson," and he struck a pose as if he had a bat in his hands and swung mightily like Casey, driving an imaginary baseball in a line drive across the Bravo into the tenements of El Paso.

Another youth, feeling his pocket to see that he still had his money asked, "How much?"

Mario smiled. At this moment he was a thousand years old and had the accumulated knowledge of every year. "Eight people—two shifts. I oney got four girls. Rain, floodin' an' wind. Some got sore throat, ches' colds, you know women. Don' know why they don' work—snash OK. Pay three dollar here, two dollar to girl. OK?"

"No," said the other. "Not okay. Too much dinero, boy. Five dollars for a little trim."

"Okay," said Mario and shrugged his shoulders. "Walk half a block it cost you twenty. Go to bar and buy drinks for girl, spen' twenty, twenty fi' dollar, then it still cost you twenty more for poosey and you get the clap. So go ahead."

In the end they settled for a twenty dollar bill between the eight. Mario and Ramón went into a small restaurant and ordered gaseosas. Mario could not sit still—Ramón found that he, also, was excited. "Did you get it all on the machine, mano?" Mario asked. Ramón had the small tape recorder on the table. Where Mario got it he did not know, but it had somehow become his task to record every conversation Mario had with gringos. He knew it was valuable because Mario had learned to speak English with it, and for the past two months he, too, had been practicing—listening and repeating, listening and repeating aloud. Mario's patience and perseverence were a wonder to him, but he had seen his friend's successes and so spent hours over the little máquina. In his pockets were two small spools, one already used, and at home he had another ten because Mario did not have a family, did not have a home, and he must keep them somewhere.

But Mario had never been as successful as he was this day. He pulled out his money and counted it. Barely noon and almost twenty-five dollars!

Ramón looked at the money impassively, but could not deny he was impressed. Mario had told him that as soon as he learned the trade, they would work together and split right down the middle. But this had not happened yet. He was learning, though, and now he even had a "job" hustling customers for two fifty-year-old girls. He pulled his own money out and it was over two dollars, as much as a grown man with a family earned for a full day's work.

Now he said, "This must for certain be a lucky day for you. Now what? Are you to try for fifty?"

"It is my lucky day," said Mario. "I knew it when I opened my eyes, but today I want to do like the rich. I want to go to the river and take a long, slow bath, then take a nap under an álamo."

It had rained for most of the week but this day was hot. There was water in the river and the canals were full. They were alone; the usual crowd of boys would not show up until four or so. They would swim for two hours and then return to the street to hustle their living. Mario disrobed quickly. He kicked his shoes off and took a running jump into the water. Ramón hesitated. He could not swim and would gradually walk in, careful to not go too far. Mario jumped around. The water was to his chest, and he called out. "Come in. Do not be afraid." He began a clumsy dog paddle, could not stay above water, and stood up. He did this twice, then said to Ramón, "Hurry, I am going into the deep part."

Ramón was in the water now, as far in as he had ever been. He was suddenly frightened. "Come back, Mario. You know you can swim no better than I can."

"Bah!" said Mario. "Dogs can swim. Will you say a dog is smarter than I am? Did any dog anywhere in the world make twenty-nine dollars this morning?"

"Twenty-five," said Ramón.

Mario laughed. "Twenty-nine. You forget that I will get fifty cents from the girls for each of the mayates."

Ramón had forgotten, and he began to formulate a reply, but Mario turned and moved toward the deep water. Ramón never saw him again.

He walked out of the water and sat naked, not feeling the hard, rocky earth. He held his head in his hands, between his knees. He shivered and felt cold, but it was hot, he knew. He was as cold at this moment as he had been a long time ago in the rock cave of the pedregal. As cold as he had been on the train coming north when they had left Mexico City. It had happened suddenly, as suddenly as all their moves had been. Chale Morgan had gone up to the centro and returned with a telegraphic money order.

"From my sister," he said. "We will go to the border and you will stay with her until I arrange for you to get across."

"You have a sister living in Mexico?" asked Ramón's mother.

"Of course," he said. "Many Americans live on this side."

That afternoon they were at Buenavista. There was only enough money for second-class fare, and a little food to last them the forty-odd hours they would be on the train. They sat in the second-class waiting room all night, for the train did not leave until early morning. For Ramón it was a pleasure trip, although the others complained about the uncomfortable seats. That night, however, it was bitter cold as the train slowly traversed the mile-and-a-half-high state of Zacatecas. And Chale Morgan covered Ramón against him, shielding him from the cold while sharing with him the warmth of his own body. "Be a good soldier. After tonight you will never be cold again in your life," he said.

The following afternoon, going through Chihuahua, Ramón would have welcomed the cold. It was unbearably hot, there was no water and there was no money for gaseosas. The car was very crowded. It was old and its windows would not open. Inside, the strong odor of unwashed bodies, defecating infants and the stale urine from the restrooms at either end of the coach made Ramón almost ill.

When they arrived at the railroad station at Juárez that night, a man waited in the shadows of the pillars that held up the roof of the platform. He was not as tall as Charlie, but had a powerful body. He came to them and put his arms around Chale Morgan. They spoke together, and Chale was smiling as they walked out to a waiting automobile.

Ramón sat in the back between his mother and Chale Morgan. After a while, Chale said, "This is a long way you are taking."

"Es que tengo un mandadito que hacer aquí," said his friend.

The driver said, "We'll get to where you want to go in a minute."

It was an ordinary street, a residential street, where they stopped. It was not very light, but Ramón could see clearly. The rear doors were opened and his mother and Chale Morgan were told to get out of the car. They stood on the sidewalk, barely three feet away from him and he could hear clearly as a new man spoke.

"¡A que mi Chale; pero qué haces aquí?"

"Pos aquí nomás, Armando," said Chale Morgan. It was the man from Mexico and Ramón had been told that he must fear him. But he had never been told why. He was not afraid, but felt a strange sensation as he watched the group alongside the car.

"¡Qué caray!" said Armando and the driver suddenly held Ramón's mother from behind and placed a hand over her mouth at the instant the friend who had hugged him drove the long knife upward and between the ribs of Chale Morgan. Ramón did not understand the words as the man said, "Charlie, mano. Remember I could always block you good?"

Now shaking from shock at the bank of the canal, he again saw Chale Morgan writhing in his death throes on the sidewalk. Twice now he had seen death, and it had come so unexpectedly, so quickly.

Once, when he had come home late, his mother, who was now drinking too much to forget her grief over Charlie Morgan, decided to exercise her authority. "Where have you been?" she shouted, surprising him with her vehemence.

"With Mario."

"I do not want you around that boy. He is too old for you to have as a friend. He is bad. He knows too much."

"He is my age, Mamá."

"Do you know what he is, what he does? Do you know he pimps for women?"

Do you know I now also pimp? he wanted to say. *Because you need money for whiskey and marihuana. I also pimp so that I can eat. And do you know that I know he has also pimped for you?* But he could only say, "He is a good friend, my only friend."

"He is too wise," she said, "too smart." And oddly she now spoke normally.

"No," he said. "He is not that smart. I am smarter than he is."

He wondered now why he thought of that time. He stood up and dressed. He took Mario's shoes and socks and put them on. Mario was the only boy on the street who wore shoes, always highly polished. Some wore huaraches but Ramón had not had anything on his feet for two years. They were a bit large, but not uncomfortable. He went through the trousers then, and took the money. In another pocket he found a small bank book. Banco Nacional—1600 pesos. He thought for a long while, then decided against trying to withdraw the money. Intuitively he knew that would be disastrous. He looked up and down the canal bank. He was very much alone. He placed the book back in the trouser pocket, then he thought of the fact that Mario had no one. He retrieved it. He picked up the tape recorder, placed the strap over his shoulder, and walked away.

At the highest point on the bridge, he stopped and looked across at the buildings of El Paso. He remained there for a full five minutes, then he walked on to stand in line. When he arrived at the turnstile, he said, "American," and walked into the new world he had selected. He was twelve years old and it was the first deliberate act of his young life. He knew from this moment he would always have something to say about his destiny.

And his only feeling of guilt about Mario was in a form of betrayal he could not explain. Mario would have been disappointed in him, for if the situation were reversed, Mario would have gone to the whores to collect his pimping fee.

NINE

At four-thirty in the morning, the old man began his work of cleaning the restrooms of the Fourth Street playground in the Second Ward of El Paso. He unlocked the doors and swept first, picking up all the refuse, then carried the waste behind the small buildings to the trashcans. It was still somewhat dark, and he carefully looked around as he worked, for he had been mugged one time but now he carried a knife. Three times in five years he had come to work to find a dead man, always young, always near the structure.

He emptied the containers into the larger cans and stood perfectly still—there, between the cans and the wall of the building, lay a form— *dead also?* he thought, *a girl? a young wino? a drug addict?*

The boy lay partially on his side, reclining against the cement, curled up holding an object on his belly, still asleep.

"¡Eh tú! ¿Estás enfermo?" asked the old man.

The boy opened his eyes but did not move. He looked at the old man with clear, expressionless eyes.

"Contéstame, tonto. ¿Estás herido?"

The boy shook his head from side to side. The old man sensed an emanation from the young boy, not fear, but something akin to resignation. He reached a hand forward. The boy reached out with his own, and pulled himself upright.

"Vente conmigo," said the old man. "Te voy a dar una mano."

"Ya me la dio," said the boy.

They walked a block south and west toward the bridge. Halfway down the second block the old man opened a door of a dirty brick building. The structure covered an entire block, each door from the street was the entrance to the living quarters of entire families—one room, one tiny kitchen area. The second floor was reached from the inner patio. Rickety outside stairs where children and grown men had fallen went up to a platform which gave access to cubicles similar to those below. Downstairs, under the stairway to save space, was one flush toilet to serve the eighty dwellings of the complex. The women washed clothes in tinas in the patio. The building had been constructed for Mexicans who had fled from their homeland to find a better life.

"Amparo," called the old man. "Te traigo tu hijo."

The boy did not object. He knew that what was now happening had been decided some time ago by someone much more powerful, more intelligent than he.

A woman, gray, but still strong, appeared. She wiped her hands on her apron as she moved forward. He put his arms around her and cried as she held him. She finally held him away for a moment and he looked into her face and said, "Aquí estoy, Mamá. Ya llegué." She asked, "¿Cómo te llamas?"

He turned to her husband. "¿Cómo se llama usted?"

"Clemente Chacón."

"Así me llamo yo también."

The woman looked past his shoulder to her husband with an expression of grief mingled with joy. They did not talk about him, they did not ask from where he came, they did not tell him of their dead son. Each knew that this was the way it must be.

Clemente Chacón went to school for one year, but he still depended upon his tape recorder, and one day he said to his family:

"Enough of schooling. I can read, I can make the letters and I know the cifras. I will help don Clemente."

Odd that he always called doña Amparo "mamá," but her husband was always don Clemente.

"Las autoridades," said the old man.

"The Government cares nothing about us." He was almost fourteen, and he could not do as well here in El Paso as in Juárez, but he could shine shoes, sell papers, run errands. "I have made myself a shoeshine kit and I will go to the plaza. If I am picked up I know English as well as my neighbors who have been in school for eight years."

"Lo que tú digas," said doña Amparo, and the old man, who had ideas about education, wanted to object but could not.

When don Clemente died three years later, Clemente mourned him as if he had been his true father, but he had never called him "papá," although he had loved him.

He had a responsibility, he knew, for doña Amparo now had no means of support, but he was now earning a living, barely, but a living, and knowing that he was really very stupid, clerking in a neighborhood corner store and making deliveries. He thought of Mario and almost heard his derisive laugh.

Even as a shoeshine boy he had been his own boss and there was nowhere to go from here, except to clerk at the 5 & 10 or to the Popular. And one day a well-dressed young man came into the store for cigarettes. Clemente was stocking the few shelves, not noticing the customer when he suddenly heard, "Ramón."

Even then he paid no attention; lost in his own thoughts the name of his past had no meaning for him. "Ramón," the stranger said again. "¿No me conoces? Soy Leopoldo Smith. ¿No te acuerdas?"

Of course he remembered him, the mozo at the restaurant, when he and Mario worked the street. But in his surprise, he was frightened and could only say dumbly, *Smith?*

But Leopoldo was genuinely pleased to see him. "Sí hombre. Smith." He switched to English. "Look man, you just never knew my apple-e-do."

"Yeah, but *Smith,*" said Clemente, and now he grinned.

"My mother married one of them," said Leopoldo, now grinning also, shaking Clemente's hand with both of his. "Twelve kids, she had, and I was the only one legal. She married one of those white nigger soldiers they got over on this side, and I was born. Guess she's still married to him since he never married the woman he has—he's one of those West Indian gray people who became an American citizen and was drafted. He had the good sense to register my birth and the paper says American so I can come and go."

"You live on this side?" asked Clemente.

"Hell, no." Leopoldo thought this amusing. "¿Pos qué crees tú? Soy mexicano. What I want with gringoland?"

"But your father? Don't you want to see him, know him?"

"Saw him once. Showed up in a Cadillac—six years old, but a Cadillac, a black Cadillac, full of calconomías so you could hardly see through the windows—Oregon Caves, Yellowstone, Grand Canyon, Acoma Village, Carlsbad Caverns, you name it and it was there. He gave my mother twenty dollars and she told him where I worked. Remember the restaurant? You were there when this happened—and he said, 'Come fer you boy. I'm taking you home.'

" 'I am home,' I said.

" 'Let's eat,' he said. 'We'll talk about it.'

"He took me to an American restaurant where a woman waited for us. She was partly white, yellow-black. Long, lean, face gap-toothed, and she tried, she really tried, and if I hadn't insisted that I was a Mexican we might have pulled it off between us, but she finally said, 'Forget it, Harold. Let him stay in this stinking hole. He doesn't want to live with white people.'

"'Now, Chrystal,' he said. 'After all, he is my kid.'

"'You got three more kids in Bloomfield.' I'll never forget that because of the way she said it, *BLOOMfield*, and he looked at me with real sadness, not knowing how much I could understand—you didn't know how much I could understand the American idiom. Mario had his machine, but I was also on the street all day and was studying in the nocturna.

"'What can I do for you boy? I wanna he'p you. Understand me?'

"'Send me twenty-five dollars a month for five years so that I can become a lawyer.'

"'OK,' he said, and that's just what he did."

"What did you do with the money?" asked Clemente.

"I became a lawyer, what did you think? Or I will be one when I pass my professional examinations and receive my credencial. Graduated yesterday—one more check, I just found out from the lawyer he hired here in El Paso. I never communicated with my father again. Everything's done through this lawyer. Good cat. Ever need a lawyer go to him—his name's Porfirio Díaz."

"Come on!"

"Yeah, really. Porfirio Díaz, Attorney-at-Law, licenciado. But I forget. Where's Mario? When you both disappeared from the street I figured you both jumped the fence."

Clemente was surprised, but knew he should not be. Who could identify a naked corpse of a thirteen-year-old after it had been in the canal a few days? "I don't know where Mario is. I came over alone and have never returned."

"Your mother thinks you're dead," said Leopoldo.

"I am," said Clemente.

"She married the taxi cab driver and left the life. She..."

"I don't want to think about that; I don't want to talk about that!" said Clemente in a harsh voice. "My name is now Clemente Chacón."

It was through Leopoldo Smith that he began to hustle again, but now in a more dangerous way. He pushed mota, at times right over the counter of the small store.

Leopoldo had returned a few months later. "Call me *Licenciado*," he said. "Any gringas you know want a divorce?" He hopped gaily. "Let my young friend off for the day," he said to the store owner. "Today I received the results of my examinations. I am a licensed lawyer."

The dark, round face of the rotund proprietor opened in a wide grin. "¿Pero, como no?" he said. "Vete Clemente, vete."

As Clemente and Leopoldo ate menudo and talked of old times, even though they had never been close friends, the young professional turned over his business to him.

"The twenty-five a month was never enough," said Leopoldo. "So I pushed shit here and on the other side. But I don't have to do that now. I don't dare do that now. I will earn money legitimately, now that I have that paper. I'm gonna handle some things for Lawyer Díaz on the other side—and I'm going into inversiones, land and insurance. But it's a natural for you if you want it."

"I can't go on the other side," said Clemente.

"You don't have to. Someone will bring it to you and collect."

"Alright," he said, and felt no guilt or fear.

It went this way for over a year. He had more money for doña Amparo and for himself, enough money finally to buy a car for himself, such as other young men he met in the same business, fast flashy cars, and he could have had the equally flashy, young Chicana girls sitting so close to the driver that they seemed as one, toking up even as they cruised the streets of El Paso's southside, but he would not, could not disregard the danger of having a car in his situation, so he did not buy one. And he did not sample his product because he had lived around it much too long and he did not envy the others the girls because he had also seen debauchery intimately and any one of those slim-shanked, big-breasted young women could have been his mother. He did not smoke yet, and he drank only an occasional beer.

But there was a sense of guilt now for what he was doing, not in a moral sense, however, because he had been calloused to this long ago. People were beyond help, sometimes. He did not even rationalize his actions by thinking that if he did not supply it someone else would. He had seen too many winos, acid heads, and junkies disappear after a few months on the street and in a few days none recalled that they had ever been there. They disappeared to who knows where; perhaps they slinked off like old, defeated cats to die where they would not be found. No, his guilt came from his own feeling of indolence, and he often thought of Mario, and again felt that he was betraying his old companion, for Mario always said, "You gotta keep hustling!" ¡A darle, bato, a darle!" And Mario had never stood still, while now Clemente did not raise a hand to make more money. The goods were delivered to him, the consumer came to him. He made a few deliveries and he was satisfied. He never roamed the streets.

And he had another worry. He saw Leopoldo Smith now and then, and although he had told him his mother must not know where he was, one Sunday morning he was home alone, doña Amparo having gone to church, when he was startled by a knock on the door.

Two young girls, extremely pretty, stood looking up at him, saying nothing. Their clothing was poor and his first thought was that they had sneaked across the border to beg or had been recruited by a zealot in Ysleta or the upper valley to distribute religious tracts, since this was Sunday.

"Well?" he finally asked.

They looked at him. One, shyly, as if embarrassed, the other very openly. "I am Caridad," said the shy one. "I am your sister, señor, and my mother sent me to tell you to come to her." She almost said Ramón, but she did not know him and her training was strong.

The weight in his chest was stifling, the fear that he could no longer remain here was mixed with an emotion that startled him. Half-consciously he reached out a hand and touched the child's cheek and he felt a deep sorrow for what she had already seen being her mother's child, and what she would yet live being a woman and he sensed another strange feeling, a very Mexican thing, responsibility for his mother's children although he had never seen one until this moment.

"You look very much like her," he said, "but I never knew about you."

"You did not want to. She took me back from where she left me when she married."

He spoke easier now. "And you?" he asked the second girl. "Are you also my sister?"

"No." She still looked at him fully, thinking, perhaps calculating.

"She is Calixta," said Caridad. "My friend."

"Queli," said the girl, giving Caridad a gentle jab with her elbow.

"Queli?" asked Clemente.

"She does not like her name," said Caridad. "Her father had a great afición for the Revolution and his apellido was Contreras but she was not born a boy so he named her Calixta. But she does not like it."

"No, I do not like it," said the other.

Clemente laughed, and he suddenly felt free of every worry he had just experienced. "But don't you think," he asked the girl, "that people will believe that your name is really Quelite and you have shortened it?"

"Oh, yes," she said, and for the first time her eyes showed real amusement, "Or perhaps, Queli importa?"

Doña Amparo came up so suddenly that he did not notice until too late. But he could not lie to her as she stood waiting to be introduced. "This is my sister, Caridad, Mamá," he said calmly. "And this is her friend, Calixta Contreras."

"Queli," said the young girl.

"Your sister!" Doña Amparo looked at him with disapproval. "And you keep her standing like this in the hot sun! For shame! Pasen niñas, pasen a su pobre casa." She behaved as if Caridad had been there often.

"Sit, sit. And there is nothing in the house to offer you." She did not remove her shawl. "I will only be a moment. Please be comfortable."

"I'll go, Mamá," said Clemente.

"No, you visit with your sister."

"Where does she go?" asked Caridad.

"For ice cream, probably. That's what she gives all the children."

"I am not a child," said Queli. But then, child-like, she smiled. "I love ice cream. I hope she gets tamarinda."

They sat, silent. Clemente went to the small sink and drank a glass of water slowly.

"Caridad," he said, "tell your mother—my mother—that it cannot be. I will never go back across—I will never see her again. You tell her that, will you?"

"Yes." She showed no emotion whatever, and Clemente was not surprised, for only he knew what he was feeling.

"And she is never to send anyone to me, not even you. You are never to come here again."

"Alright," she said. "Do you want me to leave now?"

"No," he said, and felt like a fool. "Please understand. Once I loved my mother very much. I don't feel that now. I suffered as much in other ways. I have another mother now. It is bad for me to go back. I belong here, I was born to live here on this side."

"I do not understand," she said, "but I will obey. After all, you are my older brother."

Suddenly he put his arms around her and pulled her to him. "You have suffered?" he asked harshly against her ear.

"No."

"Tell me the truth!"

"It is true. I have not suffered. Once, I suppose, when my mother gave me away to strangers I must have suffered. But I was too small to know."

"I'm glad," said Clemente. "I'm glad."

She continued. "My stepfather is a good man."

Clemente remembered the bloated taxi driver pimp. "Cipriano?" he asked.

"Yes," she said. "I call him Papá. I have taken his name since I never had one. My mother loves him very much."

"She should," he said, remembering and with a bit of jealousy. "She should, for I remember him and he was a good man."

"Everyone knows he is a good man. I go to school," she added.

He pushed her back and looked into her face in disbelief. "Truly?" he asked.

"Truly," she said. "Calixta and I are in the same class."

"Queli," said the other girl.

Doña Amparo returned and served the ice cream and small cakes. As the girls ate she wanted to ask the traditional questions. *How are your father and mother? In good health, I pray?* But she could not do so, and was ill at ease but did not show it, and asked instead, "How did you get here?"

"We walked." Caridad did the talking.

"It is not far, I hope."

"Just across the bridge."

"Across the bridge? ¿Pero cómo?"

"We just said, 'American,'" said Caridad. "It is a simple thing."

Clemente almost laughed. They rose to leave, and shook hands, seriously, like adults. Clemente reached over and kissed his sister's cheek. She reached her arms around his neck and hugged him, no longer trying to hide her feelings, weeping silently.

"¿Pero tan pronto?" asked doña Amparo, distressed. "Apenas empezamos a platicar."

"We must go," said Calixta Contreras. "Caridad only came to tell Ramón that his mother wants to see him, but he won't go." She looked directly into his eyes.

They went out quickly, and Clemente stood for a moment facing the door before he turned to face doña Amparo who stood at the center of the small room with tears rolling slowly down her cheeks.

"You must go, mi'jo," she said. "You must go see your mother. It will be as if you returned from the grave."

"I cannot," he said.

"She hurt you that much?"

"She hurt me, but that is not the reason. She hurt much more than I did. And I am not trying to hurt her now, but I cannot go back to that."

"But she is your mother, and she may need you. She may be sick."

"She does not need me that way. As a mother, yes, but not that way."

"Yet she is your mother."

"You are my mother. I can have only one mother. My name is Clemente Chacón, like my father before me. I was born right in this room years ago when he brought me to you, remember?"

She came into his arms. "You have been a good son—I could not bear to lose you, but God's will is God's will. First comes God—then we mortals follow. We cannot fight the will of God. Primero Dios."

"Do not fight it, then. I remain here."

"I am going back to the church to pray for your mother." She was composed. "You are right, probably because I want it to be that way. His will be done."

He thought now, while she was away, with mixed feelings. He felt a love for Caridad, and this did not disturb him, as his loss in her departure did not disturb him, but although, if he had expected the confrontation, he would have dreaded it, he was happy that it had occurred, for now he must act. He had known this all along and had behaved like the lazy young people around him, content to go from day to day. This would be the first and last time. He went to a far corner of the room and opened a sea chest and took the small tape recorder out and placed it on an end table. He listened for a few minutes, then carefully put it away.

He knew what he must do—take himself and doña Amparo out of the segundo barrio. This would be difficult, for she had lived there many years, had all her friends there. It would perhaps be easier to get her to discard her widow's weeds. And he must sever all connections with his former employers as well as with those who worked with him. He had some money, but he needed a job to rent a small house in another district, not too far so that doña Amparo could not come to her church or visit her husband's grave, yet far enough so that anything connecting him to the other side could never again reach him. This did not bother him too much because he had a more serious problem, and he knew there was only one way he could solve it—he must ask for help. The move would come later.

TEN

Porfirio Díaz was long and thin, and sported a ragged mustache. He was not yet fifty, but his hair was almost totally grey. His clothes hung well below his body and showed his meticulous taste, the vest, made of the same material as the suit, gave him a light conservative air. Lawyer Díaz would grow old gracefully.

"My name is Clemente Chacón..."

"How can you be? I was at your funeral," said the lawyer.

Clemente felt his entire body tremble. His face was white, and try as he might, he could not speak.

Pofirio Díaz laughed. "It's alright, boy. I know you. Leopoldo Smith told me you would be coming to see me someday."

"You scared the shit out of me, sir," Clemente blurted, then in embarrassment said, "Excuse me."

"Only a lesson," said the lawyer. "You must always be prepared when someone questions your identity. Actually you are who you are, only the name has been changed."

"I had really forgot the other name," said Clemente, "but yesterday I was remembered."

"Reminded."

"Yes, sir."

"What can I do for you?"

Clemente came to the point. "I need a birth certificate for the draft."

"That's easy, what else?"

"Then I need a high school diploma. But I don't need that until after the army."

"And why do you need a high school diploma?" asked the lawyer. "You plan to go to college?"

"No," said Clemente. "I want to get a good job."

The lawyer looked at him for a long moment. "I knew don Clemente from the time I was very young. He was a good man, a kind man, a responsible man even through the hard years. Doña Amparo is a fortunate woman to have two men such as you in her life. Leopoldo did not have to ask me to help you because I know who and what you are."

"You know who I am?" asked Clemente.

The man waved his hand as if dismissing the past. "You are the son of doña Amparo and don Clemente Chacón. You are a good son to the widow. That is all I know and it is enough. One thing about you bothers me, however, and that is the other activity—your work, not the store, but the other. You have not told me about that. What is this 'good' job you talk about? A front—you want to look respectable so that you can break the law?"

Clemente looked at him in disbelief. And the attorney misunderstood him. "You look at me, boy, as if you believe the stories my own people say about me," he said, a trace of anger came through his words and on his face was a look of disgust. "Goddamn Mexicans!" he went on. "The more you do for them, the more they criticize you. My father, may he rest in peace, told me, 'Do not worry, son, that you were born poor, for you were born a Mexican. What greater thing can there be?' And I believed him. I still do, I suppose, because the only shady things I do are done to help them. Not really shady—I've got too much respect for my profession—but things like this diploma I'm going to get for you."

He stopped and lighted a cigarette, waved the smoke away with his hand and continued talking to the amazed Clemente who wanted to speak but could not interrupt. "Do you know why I'm going to help you? Not because you're a Mexican kid who needs help, but because you're a kid who has tried to help himself. Leopoldo Smith is very astute. He is nearly brilliant, and he has told me things about you. For example, he would have never fixed that other job for you if he believed you would go deeper into that vice. As he told me when he began to push, it was but a means to an end, and with hard work he would rise above it. He was right, so I must accept that you are also of that character, but you must tell me so yourself."

"I am finished with that," said Clemente. "It is exactly as Leopoldo says—I am not lazy—I know where I am going and the sacrifices I must make."

"Alright," said Porfirio Díaz. "You had your little shortcut and you got away clean. See that it's the last one. As I said, that of the birth certificate is simple because you do not need a birth certificate. All you need is a baptismal certificate because half the Mexicans in this state never bother to register births, half of the remaining half were born in Mexico, half of whom are illegals, and the rest do not really look the way

Mexicans are supposed to look and do not even admit they are Mexicans. Our people!

"Ask doña Amparo for your baptismal certificate. She has one—there was a son, about your age."

"They never told me," said Clemente and he felt a sudden sadness. He should have guessed, should have asked, for at church, when he still went to mass with her, she had always lighted a candle to Nuestra Señora, and since don Clemente's death, she now lighted two.

"Why should they? You never told them about yourself."

Clemente did not speak.

"His name was Clemente also," said Porfirio Díaz, "and there could be a certificate of death, but I doubt it, for he died above Canutillo, in New Mexico, on a ranch where they went to pick cotton every year. Anyway, it doesn't matter. They don't check birth records against death records."

Clemente returned to Porfirio Díaz' office ten days later. "There was a baptismal certificate," he said. "And now I have a draft card. A little hassle, chewed me out some for being late, but the Board figured I was just a dumb Messican and nobody had to come looking for me, so I'm all set." He laughed.

But Lawyer Díaz did not laugh. He said, "There is no humor in taking a dead boy's identity and dragging his name through filth!"

Even now Clemente was not aware how angry the older man was. Nor did he know that it was anger mingled with disappointment and sadness. Surprised as he was, he waited and in the silence that followed, he knew he should not speak.

"You did not tell me the entire truth, Goddamn it!" The lawyer was now on his feet, waving his arms, moving his slender, expressive hands. "I knew you were frightened when you came here. Much more frightened than you should have been merely because your mother learned your whereabouts and sent your sister to you. But I didn't know how serious it was, for Christ Sake! I know where you were the day before you came to see me, I know who you were with and what was done. My information tells me not only that you were a part of it, but that you had to be. You and your friends worked for the same people. And if you were not a part of it, why protect those animals. I know of loyalty, but why are you loyal to them? I don't mean you should go to the jura and tell them, but why didn't you tell me? I can't help you, you know, if you lie to me—even by omission."

Clemente was quite calm, and it was a thing he would remember always, that he could be calm in an emergency, even though later he could fall apart. And he knew also, from the street "lawyers," that Porfirio Díaz as a lawyer was an officer of the court, and he sensed the man's integrity despite his reputation; thus he must be careful. If he left this room without speaking out, he might be in trouble. And so he spoke, also with anger, and not feigned, in an attempt to keep the lawyer from pursuing that which was most important now. "He should never have told them where I lived—Leopoldo, I mean. He knew how dangerous it would be for me to be found out."

Porfirio Díaz looked at him with disgust. "You still insist on thinking you can con me, do you? I'm going to tell you something before I kick your cholo ass out of here. Leopoldo told your mother because he was compelled to, because his mother had been a whore too, for Christ Sake! Can you understand? It was compassion for his own mother, who is now dead, that made him tell your mother what she wanted desperately to know. And now you can get the fuck out of here, buey. You gutless piece of shit—make your own way as you will!"

Clemente was white, yet he thought clearly and he knew with the instinct learned from many long years, that he had no choice. He had to tell the truth. He did not rise; still sitting in the chair before the large desk, he half-turned and raised his arms as if to ward off a blow, but his hands were open, toward the man, cutting off his words.

"I was there," he said. "And I will tell you, but first let me say this. I don't know how you know so much. I'm now convinced that you know every fact of my life—but that is all you know, facts. You do not know my feelings, my fears. You cannot possibly know my suffering..." Again he raised a hand, anticipating that the older man would speak against an appeal for special treatment because he suffered. "No me castigue porque tengo miedo—porque lo tuve, for now I am unafraid. I am not afraid of prison, I am not afraid of death, believe me. But I am afraid of losing all I have worked for. I am afraid of the end of a dream. For I have always believed, since I was old enough to think, in the American experience. I have always felt that to be here as an American was better, is better, for I still believe it, than the life I have known. It has to be, for it could not be worse. And now, when I am at the point of gaining a place here, I am also at the point of losing it all. It would not be prison, I know, because you would not hold me here and call the jura, you simply will wait until I leave and then make a phone call. But the bridge is only three blocks away, and in five minutes I would lose myself, and you would give me the time to do it because you know I did not kill anyone, you are a kind man and you are a Mexican."

Now he, too, stood up, and walked across the room. "I am young, very young, I know. And this is the reason I did not speak out when I came here the first time. I learned certain survival skills long ago. There are laws for living on the streets that you obey or perish. We learn along the way that this is also true living in a pueblo. I had a friend once, perhaps the only friend I ever had. His name was—and I don't know why I want you to know his name—Mario Carbajal. He used to put his initials everywhere, "MC," and if you go over to the Stanton Street Bridge right now, you will probably find MC's everywhere. One day I discovered that Mario was not putting his name on things at all—I knew then that he was a philosopher as well as a hustler. He was thirteen years old then, a month or two before I came across. Earlier he had already taken all the skills he knew and put them into one statement. 'Tell them nothing.' That was his most important rule of his life, and I noticed little things, because I was now learning—he carried his thinking to an extreme. When someone asked him the time of day, even though Mario had a fine underwater watch he had taken off a drunk sailor, he would say he didn't know. '¿Es que parezco reloj de pulsera?' he would ask. And then one day, this was near the last time I saw him, he told me that MC meant Meestair Craist. And all the time, if a chota stopped us, Mario forgot his name. 'Call me Pancho,' he would say. 'Everyone tells me I am called that.' 'Where do you live?' asked the quico. 'Where I find warmth,' would say Mario, then he would doblar la verga, and twist it in deep, 'Like all people born outside the rich class, the private sector or the civil servant class, I sleep where I can make myself comfortable.' Then we would get off with a light kick in the ass.

"Now Meestair Craist was a different thing. And to Mario, it was two different things—he put them together because they belonged together, but somehow he set them apart. *Meestair* to him meant money and position. He said it like the days we used the word *Don*, not like now when we call every old fart *don* because he is old. Meestair meant Americans, and they were all rich. And I remembered.

"Xochimilco. I was very small. Five, maybe six, but I don't think so. We went there—my mother, my real one, and a friend. You understand. A big man with a red beard, and later I knew he was an American. He was a friend to my mother, you understand. And earlier, it was pleasant. We had a small boat, and people came and served us food, cooking on their boats with carbón and an Indian woman came in a small canoe; she was part of the canoe because I could see nothing of her from her shoulders down, and she had flowers and our friend bought one and took it to my mother and he put it in her hair and she kissed him, I remember, the way she kissed me when I had been good, and she was so beautiful. I have not seen my mother for six years but I will always remember that—and I will always remember that she was the most beautiful thing I knew. And then we arrived at the other end where the rich people were riding horses, and there were mariachis and picnic baskets and everyone was happy—a big park with big trees and lots of grass and a huge car came near us, what they call a guayín in Mexico, a station wagon, and a man stepped out, wearing short pants; he was mostly bald, large red face, and with a belly. The children of the campesinos went over to him, '¿Se la cuido? ¿Le damos una lavadita?' looking for a small gig that would give them a peso or two, but he said, '¡No!' and turned his back to them, but he must have thought about something because he turned around to a dozen kids behind him and reached into his pockets and tossed a handful of cambio at them, who scrambled in the mud, for it had been raining, and now, his wife and children were out of the car, and the woman, blue-eyed, yellow-haired, big-assed, reached into her purse or what those things are called, as big as a red it was, and she must have saved every piece of change from the border to Mexico so that the veintes and quintos came piling out and she threw a handful on the ground. By now even adults were on their hands and knees after the pieces and then she gave some to a daughter and watched her do it, the entire family squealing with laughter as the people fought each other for the unexpected dole and then the rest of the family took turns and all were laughing but there was a little one, about two or three years old, and they put some change in his hands and he moved his arms but the money landed at his feet so that when the people went for it they tumbled him into the mud and then our friend, the bearded giant, for he was like a giant to me, went over to the man, who was laughing and making whooping noises and slapped him three times and said something to him and the man gathered his family and drove away.

"I think I understood then about Meestair and money. When Mario told me what he believed, I knew what he meant. I did not think it would be as easy to understand about Christ. But it was.

"'Craist was like money,' he told me. It was the one common thing we had, the Gringo, the rich Mexican, the gachupín, the Indian and those like ourselves, the real slaves—and he said that every Chicano in America came from our people but were now rich. The M stood for

Meestair or money, and the C, Christ, took the rap for all of us. Somehow he made us alike. He told me of a time when he went out into the street in his bare feet because it was very hot, and an American woman, an old woman, a grandmother for sure asked him, 'Child, why do you not wear shoes?' and he had a time of it deciding what to do, because he knew she would buy him at least some tenis if he played it right, but he had a perverseness, Mario did, and he decided and said, 'Christ walked in his bare feet, Ma'am,' and very nearly overcome, being from the Midwest and a Protestant, she handed him a ten dollar bill. He knew the power of Christ, but he believed more in His mother. To him Christ was very near a mita. 'Ese pinche güey nunca ha sufrido por mí,' he told me, even though his mother, before she disappeared, told him when he was small, that Christ had died for *him*, Mario Carbajal. He could not believe it in that sense, although he believed in God and would say things like, *si Dios quiere*, or *Primero Dios*; but Christ was made out to be real, like himself, and Mario could accept the idea of the llorona or of the ghosts and God, but could not accept Christ walking around hustling the streets as he did and taking punishment for everyone in any way that they might be hurt, the pimps, the whores, the hypes and the drunks, and the ordinary people of Mexico. 'You got it wrong, Mario,' I told him. 'He died for your sins.' 'What sins?' he said. 'I don' sin. You ever see me sin?' And I said, 'No,' because if he had sinned, then I, too, sinned, and I was not prepared to admit such a thing.

"'What about Jesus Christ, then?'" I asked.

"'Got a big reputation,' he said. 'Tha's all. Big reputation an' no action. I got a name on the street, no?' And he was proud of that. 'But I gotta hustle every day. I don't hustle, I got no name. This cabrón been living off a reputation for a long time.'"

"Then why is he important?"

"'Because people believe in him. He has a lot of strength. And because I should not forget this power, I write MC all over. I got MC's in every shithouse in Juárez, and once a girl I worked for wanted MF on her nalgas tattooed—one letter on each cheek, because she would be worth more to the so'jers an' sailors when they saw it and I did it with a straight pin an' ink. Put MC right on her ass, an' she never knew the difference.'

"That ended that, but Mario said, 'Tell them nothing,' and I believed him because who could disbelieve him, and I knew a man once, long before this, who trusted everyone, and he died with a knife in him, right after receiving a friendship abrazo from the man who killed him.

"That is why I did not tell you. I will tell you now."

"What happened to this Mario?"

"In the end he made a mistake. He trusted himself."

"Twice you spoke of him in the past. Why?"

"Because he disappeared. Like everyone will disappear sometime. I believe he is out of my life."

Porfirio Díaz was now quiet, thinking he had been a fool to lose his composure, for surely now he knew much more about this boy's life than the boy himself knew, and he should consider all this. He spoke with anger again, but not directed toward Clemente this time, rather at the abstract force called the system or called society. "There is very little I do not know about what happens in this filthy hole called South El Paso. In this case I do not know enough. Tell me."

"It was the day my sister came," said Clemente. "I was afraid that now I would be sent back, and I sat on the curb in front of the tenement thinking I should somehow take my mother—doña Amparo—away with me because I must go away and I could not leave her, you see. I was sitting there when the one called el Pingüino and another called Chito came along. I think this was the first time I had seen them without a car, for always they had their wheels with their fine Chicana chicks, dragging el Segundo Barrio. I never really knew them, you must understand; in fact, they must have thought I was a little weird—no woman, no car, and I did more business than they did. I rarely spoke with them except when we met to make our connection. I did not know; no one told me that there was new action in the barrio. I don't even know whether they were told to take me along. It just happened. I was there and they came by and they said, 'Quihubo,' and I said 'Aquí nomás,' and one of them said, 'Vamos a dar la vuelta.' I didn't even hesitate. I simply walked with them. If they had been in a car I would not have gone. Survival, again do you see? I could not afford to be questioned for a stupid little traffic violation, for I had no draft card. And so I walked with them and two blocks away, near the place where don Clemente found me, four or five people were talking on the corner and there were children there and Chito said, '¡Ahí está el sanavavichi!' Even then I thought nothing about it. As we came up close el Pingüino suddenly had a gun and began to shoot at a big, very handsome young man who was a stranger to me, and as the youth fell, Chito walked over with a small gun and fired three times into his head. The people scattered, and Chito and el Pingüino were running across the open playground while I kneeled there like a goddamned fool trying to help the guy, not knowing even that he was dead. I did not think of running, I simply walked home. That is what saved me until now, I suppose, that I did not run.

"That is it. No more, except that later I almost ran. To California, I suppose, because I do not want to go back to Mexico. Yet Mexico is the only place I can be safe."

"The boys confessed," said Porfirio Díaz. "Your name has not come up and there is no reason that it should. I have your high school diploma. Sonora, Texas—a wide spot on the road. It will do all that you want, except get you into college. Take doña Amparo out of the neighborhood before you become like all the rest—defeated, exploited or corrupt."

"You talk funny. You are here."

"I'm moving out also. North of Paisano to an office in a bank building. I'm going into politics because it is something I have always wanted to do and because I can be much more help to my raza. Also, because I really am a goddamn good lawyer. Don't worry too much about that other trouble. I do not think the familia will let you down."

"Everything is in order, then?" Clemente could barely believe it had been so simple.

"Have my secretary make photostats of your draft card, the baptismal certificate and the diploma. I will get you a delayed birth certificate, then you can really be an American. So legal, in fact, that if you develop a little more larceny in your soul, you qualify to be President of our great country."

"I have to thank you," said Clemente. "I am but a child in these matters..."

"You are conning me again," said Porfirio Díaz, and this time he smiled. "Because I can't let you get away with it, I must tell you. I had very much affection for Chale Morgan."

The Army did not want Clemente Chacón. The years of privation in his early life had left him with a deficiency that, while not serious, made him imperfect for the service except in the time of war. And soon he was on the street, selling cold from house to house cheap silverware and plastic kitchenware.

One day he moved doña Amparo out of the Segundo Barrio across the real boundary that separated brown from white to a small cottage on Aurora in the Highland area. Clemente Chacón was on his way.

ELEVEN

Clemente Chacón sat at his desk, asleep. Lucinda Gray came into the office and quietly reached over and switched off the tape recorder. She had seen it a number of times, but she did not know about it, did not know the reason it existed, did not question.

Clemente woke with a start. He had not meant to fall asleep, and he rose and walked into his washroom. He splashed cold water on his face, then looked at his reflection in the mirror, trying to find some evidence in his features of the soreness he felt. He was in real pain now that his body had relaxed for a time. He dried his face and combed his hair, then walked out of his office, through the foyer to Mr. Smith's office. Virgil was not there but that was not important, since all he sought was company for a few minutes. Mrs. Knickrem looked up at him and smiled.

"Mr. Smith thought you were in Juárez for lunch, so he joined Mr. Calhoun at his hotel for an hour or two. He said something about a nap after that—before the evening's festivities. Something I can do?"

Clemente smiled in return, shook his head, but did not speak. He walked along the large room. A man sat across from Miss Gray. He wore Levis, too small for him, scuffed shoes, unmatched socks, and a sweatshirt with the legend, 'DON'T LITTER' across the chest. It was baggy and dirty. On his knee was a beret and his hair fell over his eyes and ears. Clemente glanced at him as he walked into his office. Lucinda followed him and closed the door. For a minute he stood at his window, looking down to the parking lot. Along the sidewalk a girl walked, the wind doing things to her short skirt. He turned and looked at Lucinda with that incredulity he always had when he could leave his role as her boss, with appreciation and pleasure—as a man, not lasciviously, but with a sheer joy that he could look upon her loveliness, and he was unaware that she resented his objective point of view.

"Your lieutenant must have been blind," he said. "Why are you here, Lucinda?" He had called her Lucy once, and she had objected. "You should be in a *Playboy* centerfold, or in motion pictures, or married to a broke European prince."

She was angry suddenly. "There are more important things, Mr. Chacón."

"I'm sorry," he said. And he smiled. "I guess I'm not very good with women. I never say the right thing. But I mean no harm."

She was immediately contrite. She had sounded like Ruth Knickrem, she thought. He had paid her a sincere compliment and she had been brusque because she was so much in love with this man. Never in their relationship had he made a leading remark, an off-color suggestion, anything that would tell her she was less than a lady in his eyes, and if he had she would not have the deep respect she had for him, yet she wanted something more. She wanted to be respected, yet she wanted him to desire her.

And she had not forgot that of this morning, although she knew he had pushed it out of his mind, and she could still taste the inside of his mouth and was embarrassed that she had done that which she could not help doing and was now embarrassed because she remembered it with pleasure. But she was not a prude, and she had been ready when Mr. Smith put his hand up her dress that one time, and had taken his wrist strongly, then sat carelessly, exposing leg and thigh, on the corner of his desk and spoke to him in his language. "You can fuck Ruth all you want, but keep your Goddamn hands off me."

"Don't be careless," said Virgil Smith. "It isn't difficult to find secretaries."

"It *is* difficult to find competent secretaries, Mr. Smith. I was never told that my job description called for me to open my legs to you. If that is the case, you must accept my notice now, but first bring in Mr. Chacón so that you can explain the reason for my resignation, since he, of course, is involved."

Virgil Smith became expansive. "Clem is involved? Well. Goddamn, girlie. He has out-Virgiled Virgil. And I've always told him one should never dip his pen in company ink. So he's been punching you all this time with no one the wiser. Son of a bitch! And I always believed he was so square. He doesn't even like dirty jokes!" And he laughed with pleasure. "OK, let's forget this little charade. I didn't know I was moving in on someone else's territory. We'll be mature about this—there's no need for Clem to know."

No, there had been no need for Clemente to know. She understood this in her frustration because this human slug of a man could never understand that Clemente's integrity was so far superior to his, that if Clemente knew, Virgil Smith would not only lose out on a piece of ass, but would also lose his top executive. She knew what Clemente had done in the past year—over a million dollars of group insurance aside from his countless debit men scattered all over El Paso and Isleta. It was some time before Virgil knew that he had been allowed to believe something that was not true.

Now she moved toward Clemente, and she touched him. He cringed, and she said, "No, Clem. It is I who should be sorry." Her hand was on his upper arm. "And please, if only for a moment, let me touch you. That is all I will ever have of you, you see. This has turned out to be one hell of a day. I'm still not over those thugs beating you this morning. I'm sorry."

She thought other things as he spoke and she did not hear his words. She had no recollection of her ever having a prejudice in her life, and she was compelled to think of it now. Growing up in the Army, there were Negroes, now called Blacks, called niggers even by each other, and there were problems, not because they were Negroes but because they were a people somehow set apart. As far as her father was concerned, the problems were because they were Black and he had to be concerned with them. And to him, yes, they were inferior! She heard many arguments, the rhetoric of the high command, those who train them but would not lead them into battle; but her country was a democracy and she attended school with the enlisted men's children and made friendships that somehow wore away. Her sin was not thinking about it, so perhaps she did have the same prejudices as her people.

And now she was in love with a Mexican, a Mexican married to a Mexican whom he loved and would not have a mistress, which she had decided she would do even if she did not work at getting this done, and her parents if they knew would believe that he would divorce his wife in a minute, not for love of another but to marry into a better class. They truly believed that Mexicans believed themselves to be inferior because they had spent so much time making them believe that they were. How would he feel, her father, to know that this man would not have her even as a mistress? He would never believe it.

Looking at Clemente she remembered Huachuca. She was very young, yet she remembered the honey wagons. The latrines, outhouses that must be cleaned out at least once a month and the detail was composed of Mexicans and niggers. Trucks were loaded with shit, to be taken out to the desert and dumped. The driver was always an Anglo-Saxon, blue-eyed, but the workers were from the nether area of society. And she saw, looking at him as a buck private shoveling feces, and suddenly one tear came from her right eye and she thought incongrously that it should be from her left eye because it was weaker. She knew then that she must tell him what he would not accept.

Again she said, "I'm sorry. Let's get on with it. How do you feel?"

"I'm alrigh'," said Clemente, reverting to his childhood speech. "Who's that guy out there? Virgil hiring a new janitor?"

Now she laughed. "That's your man, Clem. You called him."

"Villegas?"

"Yes."

"Christ! I guess I have to talk to him since he's here, but Goddamn! The Senator has played me a very dirty trick!"

"You'll be surprised, Clem. We had a good talk while you slept. He's sexy," she could not help adding. "I said that you were asleep, and I don't know why I told him that, really, and he said, 'Why doesn't the son of a bitch sleep at home.'"

"He really talked like that? Christ! For a guy that's looking for a job..."

"Then he said, 'My time is valuable,' and he pulled a dollar watch out of those dirty jeans of his and looked like he was on his way to an IT and T board meeting."

"OK, bring him. I have to go in a minute. Did you talk to the Senator?"

"He's here. But he is busy most of the day." She looked at her pad. "I have every stop he will make so I can reach him in a few minutes if anything should come up. He's even going to the University to talk to your friends."

"What friends?"

"Those three of this morning. The MOCOS."

"MACHOS," he said, and laughed.

"That may be, but they're MOCOS to me." She paused and there was merriment in her eyes. "Who is Evangeline, Clem? Is it something I should not know?"

He said quickly, "Did she call? Is there anything wrong?"

She realized he was really concerned and was sorry she had joked. "No, only the Senator said he will be with her at five and hoped you could meet him there."

"She is a very old friend, a very dear friend," said Clemente, his face serious. Then he added, "Something like a grandmother."

She said, "I'm taking at least three minutes of Mr. or Doctor..."

He looked at her incredulously.

"Villegas' time. I must talk to you."

"He's a doctor?"

"Yes." She sat down, and suddenly nervous, smoothed her skirt on her thighs. "I know you want me at the ceremonies tonight, and I would do so if I believed I am needed as your secretary. But I am not and will not attend. Certainly if you would order me to do so, I would be there. I have never met your wife. I have avoided it. Early, I suppose it could have happened, but there came a time when I did not want it. I must confess that I have seen her. When she comes here, which is rare, and once I followed her to the A&P and saw her and your son, Pete. She is a most beautiful person."

She loved the fact that he was a dull man. "You mean I have never presented her to you?" he asked, at this moment becoming Mexican in speech and thought.

She looked at him and shook her head. She was becoming angry at his denseness. "You had other things on your mind, Mr. Chacón," she said with sarcasm. "And if she noticed me, she had nothing to worry about because she is certain of your fidelity." He would have spoken but she stopped him with a gesture. "But you must know that I love you. And I also deserve a celebration tonight. You have never been to my place. I know you feel it would be wrong. Perhaps I have not hidden my feelings well enough. But I want you to stop by tonight and bring your wife—not for protection, because you don't need that. I want you to stop in tonight if only for a short while because I will never again see you in my apartment, around my things, the objects I love. This will never happen again because, you see, I am leaving you."

"No," he said, sensing her reasons. "That isn't necessary, unless you don't want to be here anymore."

"I cannot be around *you* anymore. And I must talk about that which you refuse to see. I love you, and I must go. It isn't as simple as I make it sound, but it's the way it has to be. You must understand that it was only today that I knew this. Today it was not a sexual thing that made me put my tongue into your mouth. It simply had to happen. I was concerned for you, I suffered with you, but I didn't know until then how deeply involved I've become with you."

He was moved and somewhat sad; as if in pain he said, "I didn't know—I don't really understand. We are together a great amount of time, we like each other, work well together but I have never been aware of doing anything to make you uncomfortable..."

"Perhaps that is one reason why I fell in love with you. I have never been uncomfortable with you because you are an honorable man." They looked at each other for a long moment without speaking, without a word remaining to be said. When she finally spoke, it was in her business tone. "When you return from Boston, I'll come in until you find a suitable replacement for me. I'll type out my formal notice while you speak to Mr. Villegas."

He, too, spoke once more, "I'm very sorry, Lucinda."

She did not smile. "I know you are, and it's not your fault at all. It isn't *our* fault at all."

The man sitting before him had been speaking for a few minutes, but Clemente had not heard a word. His mind was on Lucinda, but also on his life, and for the first time he doubted his success. He looked at the man, and realized that his gaze for a time had been fixed on the other's neck, and along the hairline, where there were obvious traces of dirt. He was suddenly attentive, and his look shifted to the man's face, the stubble of beard, the bleared cast to his eyes, and suddenly also, he knew not why, he asked, "Do you drink?"

"Like a fucken fish," the man said and laughed. But he saw that Clemente was not amused, so he added, "No, that's not quite right—not if you take it literally. I don't drink any more than the next person. These rings under my eyes are inherited from my mother, a beautiful lady who never had a drink in her life. You know, the Prince of Wales, if he is still alive, has them also. And also inherited, all the way back to Queen Victoria. But I answered in that way, I suppose, because I believe, perhaps, that we all drink too much." And yet he knew that he had answered in that manner to shock Clemente into listening to him. "However," he said now seriously, "you are obviously not prepared to talk to me now. I can come back at any time, just let me know." Oddly, to Clemente, his voice sounded kind.

"No, no," said Clemente. He waved his arm as if to break away from other thoughts. "I'm sorry. I don't usually make excuses, but I have had a difficult day."

"As I said," the man continued, "we can talk another time." He stood up, prepared to leave.

"It must be now," said Clemente, somehow attracted to this unusual person, very much aware that he had in the beginning sought a way to get rid of him, and now wished that he would remain with him no matter what. "On Sunday I leave for Boston, and if you're our man, you'll come with me."

"I'm here cold, you know," said the man. "The lad you sent said there might be a job for me here, so I came. What do you want, what do you need?"

"Mr. Villegas," said Clemente, and his voice did not show how tired he was, "this is a crazy day and this is a crazy interview. You've been recommended to me—very highly recommended—to take over my PR program. To set one up, actually, because I don't have one. I don't mean to be insulting, but looking at you I am thinking that we are both victims of a horrible practical joke. Since the person who recommended you is not vicious, you must know him intimately. Please accept my word that I had nothing to do with this. You will be recompensed, of course, for your time and your trouble."

"¿Todo se arregla con dinero, verdad?"

"What do you mean?"

"Well, I came here, away from important things, and it turns out to be a joke. So you make it right by giving me money for my time. That is all! Big fucken deal! Listen, you pay me only when I do a job for you. My time cannot be paid for with money. You have to do better than that. You must pay, perhaps, a greater price—like your friendship, for instance. Something that might require a little effort on your part."

Clemente looked at the man and felt ridiculous because they had gone beyond sparring when he had been prepared to dismiss him out of hand. He sensed a strength in the man, but he was also strong, and he said:

"I've told you. I have an opening and you have been recommended. I have nothing to do with interrupting your important business; you could have refused to come here. Tell me what you have done and if you can take this assignment. Let's stop fucking around."

"Alright, we'll stop fucking around," said Natividad Villegas, "but I must tell you that I had to come here. Not only because I need a job but because you interest me. I know who you are and I mistakenly assumed you knew about me. The lad said you wanted me right away, so I came as I was—I was doing yard work."

"You know about me?" asked Clemente, genuinely interested in how this man could possibly know him.

"Not much, really. I know who you are, what you do, a little about your work history, age, wife, Calixta, one child, Peter."

"But how?" And Clemente smiled, surprised and curious.

"There's a list, you know," said Natividad. "I saw it in San Francisco when I was researching a series of articles in Berkeley—all the great, near great, and potentially great Chicanos are on it, with a brief biography."

"Are there really 'great' Chicanos?"

"It depends, I suppose, on how one defines, 'great' or 'Chicano.' Our brothers who made up this list mean success—they speak of those of us who have made it, on their terms, in the *white man's* world. But the list isn't all of it. There is a book, too, a regular Who's Who in Chicanoland. You're not in it though."

"And you are?" asked Clemente, still smiling, relaxing for the first time this day.

"No. I couldn't afford it. Costs twenty-five bucks to be in it, and you have to provide your own photograph. Another fifteen bucks. You get a special edition, though, bound in crocus or something."

"And what is it for?"

"I'll be goddamned if I know. First of all, however, it's a money-maker, but beyond that it must be some kind of propaganda. It serves as an example to young Chicanos. If they work hard, then they can grow up to someday appear in the book, if they can come up with forty dollars. ¡Ay qué mi raza!"

"It might not be a bad idea," said Clemente, "to make the other side aware that our people are capable of contributing to our society, that we don't lack the intellectual capacity to become lawyers, doctors, educators."

Natividad laughed. *"The other side!* You don't really believe there is another side, an enemy. You wouldn't be where you are if you can believe that."

Clemente was confused. No, he did not believe that, but why had he said it? All his life he had sought knowledge; he had never turned away from a situation or a conversation that could teach him something.

"Some time ago," said Natividad, "before my time, even, a number of leading psychologists, doctors and anthropologists wrote articles and even books proving that we are inferior. There were diagrams illustrating the shape of our skulls, drawings of our shovel-shaped incisors, statistics proving our ability to withstand the rays of the sun and how our inferior bone structure enabled us to work at stoop labor for hours on end without our tiring.

"Now, there are two very important things here. The first is that we are not singled out for this treatment. The Negro and the Oriental, in short, those ethnic groups that supplied cheap farm labor for the land barons, especially in California, were labeled and categorized in an effort to keep them in ignorance. The Oriental, in fact, had it worse because the clergy joined in to add paganism to their inferiority. The second point is that not all these experts were bigots. A few were, of course, but

101

the majority sold their reputation for money. These persons were not only dishonest, but because they had pretensions toward scholarship, they were immoral.

"I made these two points because they are very evident in the teachings of Chicano leaders. Overtly or not, young Chicanos are being taught to believe that our people are the only people in America who suffer, or that they suffer more than any other group. The young are also being led into a state of mass paranoia. *They're all against us!* has now become a state of mind. A great conspiracy in Anglo America is out to get us simply because we're Mexican. Ironically, some of our young people are bound to believe that it is *true*. That we *are,* in fact, inferior. And their plea for equality becomes a lament—we are creating a generation of crybabies. Christ! I know that the majority of us are oppressed, starved, suppressed, exploited, fucked over time and time again. But those of us who are rich or in the upper-middle-class income level or even those in the middle class who are buying their own home and have a steady job are not. So it has nothing to do with race.

"But shit, I'm talking too much. I suppose I miss the classroom."

"Go on. Tell me more," said Clemente. "I guess I need classroom work."

"There is a third point here, perhaps the most important, and our people refuse to see it. This entire situation is a matter of economics. We are necessary as a work force. And believe it, it is scientific as hell if we are all to survive. *We,* or *any* people who provide a source of cheap labor must be kept in that situation. Some of the scholars I spoke of wrote their lies for money; this is natural and that is where it all begins. Racial bigotry is the result of an economic condition. History is full of this.

"As for your comment about showing the other side how great we are, the only people who will see that book are those who appear in it and their friends. Really, who gives a good shit about a Chicano becoming a lawyer? Other Chicanos. Why? Because they have been conditioned to believe that this is an exceptional accomplishment. Brainwashed to believe we *are* inferior, and it is the greatest mistake we can make, to keep our people in ignorance, helping this by making something extraordinary out of what should be the norm. Why in hell shouldn't we produce doctors and lawyers and architects? Mexico is full of them as well as painters and poets and writers. And the same blood that courses through their veins courses through ours. There is something sick about us, a deep-rooted mass insecurity that drives us to near megalomania simply to prove we are as good as the enemy, the 'other side.' "

Clemente said, "You seem to be pretty emotional about all this. I've never thought about it that much, though I am very sensitive to the plight of the Chicano."

"You're goddamned right I'm emotional but that is because I'm pissed off! We seem to be doing this in the wrong way, this business of having the opportunity of upward mobility. And what is upward? And do we trade off this opportunity for our integrity, our honor and the fact that we are *men*? Are we to become crybabies like a good portion of our Negro brothers have done, *You owe it to us, Whitey, you motherfucker! You been fucking us over for about three centuries, Ofay! Now YOU pay up!* Believe it or not I have heard the words, a bit different, but the substance was the same, from Mexican militants. It seems to me that now, only the Indians—now called 'Native Americans'—have retained their pride. They're not out for the dole; those sonsabitches fight. And the plight of the Chicano you speak of lies within himself. But how could you think about it very much? You're busy becoming what you are and your personal success is another statistic to be used. And yet, what you and I have done is a good thing. Not to prove we are capable but to show that it can be done by *anyone*. And now, alas, to prove to *our people* and not to the 'enemy' that we can do it.

"But you are right. I am involved, not only emotionally, however. I have been in the movement because I have been a teacher. I am still part of it, but I become so frustrated and angry that sometimes I wish I had never heard the word *Chicano*. As I said, I know of inequities. In the slums and in the rural areas. Yet, I have also seen our Chicano brothers work unceasingly to help elect a Nixon. At political rallies, I have seen clean-cut Chicano youths manning hospitality suites at political gatherings for Ronald Reagan—Christ Sake! Mod groomed, impeccable, healthy, smug, their very appearance somehow representing their utter disregard for the lack of social progress, passing out expensive scotch and equally expensive literature. I felt betrayed, somehow, as I did the first time I saw a Mexican homosexual. To me, Mexicans are somehow above such things. In the end, such experiences strengthened my belief in equality."

And now he seemed to leave the scene, thinking, remote, and he said, "Anyway, you want to know about me, what I have to offer. I'll be brief. B.A. Stanford, M.A. Emory, Ph.D. Berkeley. Parents Mexican peones, migrant workers, crop followers. I've done PR. Lend me your phone and we'll get the right recommendations."

Clemente said, "All that, and you're out of work?"

"I work all the time. Right now I'm trying to prove Tasso's influence on the development of the short story. At the moment I'm out of a salaried position, which isn't that important. I always make out."

Clemente was finished. "I must accept that you know what you have to do. Anyway, we'll find out soon enough. Ten thousand to start plus expenses. Limits on the last will be decided later. In three months your base salary will go to thirteen, after that it is up to you. We work all day tomorrow and leave for Boston on Sunday. I've a press conference at six tonight. Be there to listen in. Banquet tonight, also—etiqueta—please bring your wife." He buzzed, and Lucinda came in. "My secretary, Miss Gray," he said, although she had already talked to him. "She'll have some papers for you to sign." To Lucinda, he said, "Find a desk for Mr. Villegas—something temporary. When Mr. Smith leaves for Los Angeles, Mr. Villegas will have his office. I'll remain here. Show him around and get him a girl from the pool. Work out an ad for the papers—he'll need help—young person, the best, greaser, chink, Jap, nigger, honky or broad. Makes no difference. Call Boston for two more rooms, and send someone downstairs for more cash. You're both going with me. Call the airlines, too, of course."

"Yes, Mr. Chacón." Lucinda waited.

She looked at Clemente, questioning. Then he understood. "Give Mr. Villegas cab fare from petty cash." He returned to Natividad, with a look that was unmistakably apologetic. "Do you need money now?" he asked.

Natividad Villegas smiled, and could not hide his amusement. "No, Mr. Chacón. I have the proper attire."

"Very well," said Clemente. He took a key and opened the drawer where he kept the tape recorder. He took a bank deposit book and dropped it into his jacket pocket.

It was a dismissal, and Villegas understood. He stood up, and again there was amusement in his eyes. "Okay," he said. "We'll do it for a while."

TWELVE

That year, when Charlie Morgan returned to El Paso after El Cajón, his father died, but not before he saw his one remaining son come through in the manner of his older brothers, in the manner of the Morgans. Although he would never admit it, even to himself, Charlie was the only disappointment the old trooper had had in his life. But now his son was a different person.

George Morgan could not explain how Charlie had changed, yet he knew, and he said to his wife, Evangeline, "Micah done good with the boy. Straightened 'im out real good. Wouldn' be surprised if he got 'im fucked while he was out there."

Evangeline straightened the antimacasser behind his head and patted him gently on the cheek. She tolerated her beloved husband's obscenities, nevertheless remained a lady, and said, "Most likely, the boy grew up in the past weeks. Maybe he even found his peace with the Lord." Although she was not overly religious, she was God-fearing.

George Morgan almost grimaced. In the Calvary one did not look to the Lord. One looked after his horse and his gear. The animal was many times more important than family. "No," he said. "he's knowed a woman out there. I was beginning to worry about m' boy."

She smiled a secret smile, knowing her George, bow-legged, little George Morgan, with an upper torso of a six-footer, a thrice broken nose from his innumerable brawls, who still believed that being with a woman was the making of a man, who had never, she knew, had a woman other than her, because, and this unknown to her, he could not perform unless he was with a virtuous woman and what she did know was that despite his brusque manner and bad language he was always tender when making love. She did not know, either, that with her son it would be exactly the opposite. She smiled in pleasure and then she remembered a thing in the long past, and she turned away as pain contorted her features, and when she composed herself she went to him and kissed him, surprising him as he sat with the American Legion

Newsletter in his hands, the antimacasser again awry, and said, "I'm so glad you married me."

He was uncomfortable. "Why, I'm glad, too, girlie," he said. After a moment, "Coach tells me Charlie has a good chance to make the team," he said and grinned.

"You like that, do you?" she asked. "I don't know that I do. Football is a very rough sport. Football and wars. It seems that is all my life has been. Football and wars."

"We gotta be proud, girlie," said her husband. "We had Morgans in every war our country's ever had. An' Morgans died, too, from way back in the beginnin' in No'th C'lina, they tell me, and they was all calvary. A General even, onc't. I know you're thinking of our boys, but we been patriots an' Charlie's no different." He seemed almost unhappy that there was no war for Charlie. But George Morgan died before Korea and did not live to be disappointed in his one remaining son. He had known disillusionment in the military during the Second War when horses had been made obsolete by the jeep and he had loved to say at American Legion dances, "Imagine the look on ol' Schickelgruber's face when he sees 20,000 troopers comin' at 'im with bugles ablowin' an' flags flyin'."

"We's so'jers," he said to his wife. "An' it gripes my ass to see things changin'."

Charlie Morgan went out for football that fall, but not with his father's idea that he had a chance to make the team. "I'm not going to be on the bench long," he told Coach Humphreys. "I come to play, and if I don't have the ability, tell me and I'll go away."

Hump Humphreys, All-Southwestern end fifteen years ago, but now with a belly like a medicine ball, said, "Ah lahk yo' sperit, bo'. Ah got bo's heah bein' paid to play 'cause college coaches are interested in 'em. Lahk ah say, ah lahk yo' sperit, but yo' plays when I tell you."

"Fuck you," said Charlie Morgan. "I'm not asking for any favors, but I'm staying."

Humphreys walked away, hiding a grin, thinking that maybe his luck had changed and he had found a good one all by himself. He was not concerned that the boy had spoken to him in that manner, did not think that if he had done that in high school he would have been expelled. But football was no longer a sport but a business. And he played the game.

It was not until the third quarter of the first game that Charlie was allowed to play, and it was on the first play that he took over the Austin High School football team. The quarterback called a play and Charlie said, "No. Let's counter." They took a five yard loss for delaying the

106

game, and he walked to the quarterback who was looking to the sidelines and said, "I'll punch you out right here if you call time." He sent the wingback through the line against the flow of the play for twelve yards, then from his tailback position, he kept the ball and raced sixty-seven yards through a broken field for a touchdown. "Good playcallin'," Coach Humphreys said to the quarterback. He did not even glance at Charlie.

The following day word came from Austin. A University alumnus talked to Humphreys. "Coach says to play him," he said, and Charlie started every game after that.

He had noticed Shauna Stafford while sitting on the bench, as almost deliberately she moved before him, spinning, tossing her short skirt, showing her tight little ass under cheerleader's tights, and as he moved to the waterbucket, he said, "How about a 'burger and a coke after?" and she hardly looked at him and said, "OK." He was not certain he had heard her, but she was waiting when he left the dressing room where all the girls waited for their boyfriends, and very naturally he took her hand and led her to his old man's Edsel. He stopped for a light and she pointed to a Gunning and Casteel on the corner. "Don't you think you ought to stop?" she asked.

"What for?"

"To get some rubbers, silly. I'm not gonna do it unless you use a safe." And thus it began with Shauna, then later Elaine, Isabel, Sara and a fragile, winsome Jewish girl named Michelle. He fucked them all, but most of his spare time was spent in Juárez, in a crib with a forty-year old mother of ten children.

It was during the last game of the year, a playoff game against Bowie, an all Mexican school, that he met Lázaro López. Lázaro was sixteen years old, all shoulders, five feet ten inches, one hundred seventy-nine pounds of intuitive football player. All afternoon he knocked Charlie down with vicious body blocks. After the game, he came into the dressing room to congratulate Charlie, who had finally gone to the side opposite Lázaro to score the winning touchdown.

"Jesus Christ," said Charlie. "Nobody ever teach you how to tackle, mano?"

"I can tackle alright," said Lázaro. "Gotta practice blocking' though. Don't expect to grow much more; too small to be a defensive lineman in pro football. Gonna be one of those little 200-pound running guards. What you doin' after? Wanna come with us to Juárez for a little fun?"

"Gotta date," said Charlie.

"So—bring your chick. We're all taking our snatch with us."

Charlie's life in Juárez really began here. Lázaro knew places and people. And when Lázaro did not go with him, Charlie went alone to a night club where he was now known and liked.

In January, he and Lázaro López went to San Antonio, the only players from El Paso to play in the North-South game. They were more than a little frightened, but it did not matter because they played only a few minutes near the end, when the game had already been decided. They returned to El Paso, wearing their game jackets, carrying souvenirs, and they vowed that they would return to Houston, where the game would be held the following year, and show them something.

Strangely, Charlie did not miss his father, who had died just before Christmas. He thought of him with regret only when he achieved a personal victory. He was still growing, and that year he batted .460 for the varsity, ran a .49 flat quarter and 1:59 in the 880 for the track squad. By fall, even though he was only a junior, he was watched by scouts from every major conference.

That season, he and Lázaro carried their feud on the field as their friendship grew in the nightclubs and brothels of Juárez. He was somewhat of a celebrity on the other side, for some of his Mexican friends came across the river to watch him play. And he and Lázaro both went to Houston, where he played well. Charlie did not win an award, but he felt as if he had because Lázaro was named best defensive lineman.

On their return, at a party given in their honor by friends from across the border, Charlie Morgan became a pimp. He and Lázaro crossed a line that they would never recross. Although mixed couples—Mexican, non-Mexican—were still taboo in El Paso, Lázaro, as a star athlete, was now more often seen with non-Mexican girls in non-Mexican groups.

Charlie took Shauna, who was always ready and whom he knew to be game for anything that might come up. Lázaro had a dark-haired, green-eyed fifteen year old named Marsha who was a little on the heavy side, for Lázaro liked heft in his women.

The party was at a nightclub, the food was good, and the drink was plentiful. Armando, who was but a few years older than they and had become their good friend, acted as host and introduced them to two men, both in their late fifties.

"Don Pedro Villa and Juan Pablo Ordóñez," he said to the boys. "They are visiting us from Mexico City."

"Mucho gusto," said Charlie, taking the older man's hand.

"The pleasure is mine," said don Pedro in very good English.

Later, Charlie realized that no one in the party was smoking. "You notice anything, mano?" he asked Lázaro.

"Yeah," said Lázaro. "Looks like they clean run out of yesca." And once, Shauna, returning from a dance with one of the Mexican men, said in a loud voice to Charlie, "When am I gonna get a little toke, honey?"

"Shut up," he told her in a harsh whisper. He sensed there was something different here, and looking at Lázaro he knew his friend was also uncomfortable, and then don Pedro called him to come sit by him.

"I understand," said the man, motioning to the waiter for more drinks, "that you are an excellent athlete. I was better than average in my youth, but in *our* game of fútbol. I've never been able to see anything in your game, but I'd like to come and see you perform sometime if I'm visiting during the season."

Charlie laughed, and he liked the man. "It is not a performance, sir. It's a game—we play."

Don Pedro also laughed. "Always there is difficulty with the idiom," he said, deliberately sounding as if the words were in Spanish. "But am I invited?"

"Certainly," said Charlie.

Don Pedro handed him the fresh drink. "That little girl you brought tonight," he said, and his eyes looked shrewdly into Charlie's face. "How old is she?"

"Almost sixteen," said Charlie, forgetting for a moment that she was passing for eighteen, and he felt a sensation in his chest that moved down toward his groin. He knew suddenly what the man was after, but waited for him to say it, knowing that he would agree only if he said it in the right manner, and also knowing it would happen because the man was not evading his look which would have somehow made them both dirty.

"I want to fuck her," said don Pedro. "Can you fix it?"

"I can fix it," said Charlie, certain that he could talk Shauna into it.

"You're very mature for a teenager," said don Pedro. Charlie shrugged. "I will pay, of course," the man added.

"Don't spoil it," said Charlie. "This one's on me."

"I insist," said don Pedro. He spoke to Charlie very seriously now, almost as if he were giving him a message rather than advice. "Never give away for nothing what you own. I'm in business and I never break that rule."

"But I don't own her."

"If she will do what you say, you own her."

Charlie felt a slight chill. "As you wish," he said. "But I meant what I said. After all, it never wears out."

"Oh, but it does," said don Pedro, still serious. "It does wear out, and when it does, then is when you should discard it or give it away. It is useless then." Now he smiled. "And the other, the Chicano there, will his women do it also?"

"I don't know," said Charlie.

"Talk to him, will you? My friend, Juan Pablo, likes a meaty backside. But right now I am thinking he is out of luck, for that young man will not agree."

"Because he is Mexican?" asked Charlie, feeling somehow insulted.

"No," said don Pedro. "Because he is dangerous."

But Lázaro did not object, and Shauna and Marsha went laughing up the stairs with the two older men while the party continued and no one thought a thing about it.

"Who is he?" Charlie asked Armando.

"Mr. Villa? He's many things, but mainly, he's my boss. He owns the place." He then took out a billfold and gave each of them a fifty dollar bill. He added two twenties, one for each of the girls.

"You knew this would happen all along," said Lázaro, and he was angry.

"Not when I planned your celebration—I did not invite you here for this," said Armando quickly. "It all happened tonight, while we have been sitting here."

Charlie felt somewhat like Lázaro, as if he were being used, but he was not angry. If Armando said it was so, it was so.

"He wants both of you to work for him," said Armando. "Bring young gringas over two or three times a week. Not here, one of them might get hurt sometime and you would be in trouble. A more discreet place he owns outside of town. Open only to club members—professional men, bankers, no tourists, no Americans. The Mexican likes a güerita now and then, especially a young one, just as the gringo likes our young beauties."

Charlie did not speak and Lázaro asked, "How much?"

"A couple of hundred a week for each of you, sometimes more. A hundred for the girls, or whatever you want to give them."

"I'm on," said Lázaro, and Charlie nodded his head, still not speaking, thinking.

Lázaro asked, "How come there's no grass here tonight?"

"Don Pedro doesn't allow us to use it. Only street pushers can smoke, he says."

"He owns them, too?"

Armando shrugged and smiled. "Who knows?" he said, then seemed to reach a decision and asked, "Want to sell for us on the other side?"

"No," said Charlie, finally speaking. "We can't fuck around with that." But Lázaro did not answer, and Armando knew he would speak to him alone later. He also knew that the Mexican boy needed money more than Charlie did.

"All set, then," said Armando. "Come over tomorrow or whenever you can and I'll take you out to the place. Now how about a little fun. I didn't have anything ready for you because you were bringing dates, but we got a couple of new ones in today. Mr. Villa brought them from Mexico City, as a matter of fact. What do you say?"

"Christ," Charlie said to Lázaro. "They import them from Mexico as if there weren't enough whores in Juárez already."

"They weren't behaving very well down there," said Armando. "Juárez is a demotion for them."

"I'm ready," said Lázaro. "Come on, Charlie."

"Not me, mano," said Charlie. "You go ahead."

Armando was suddenly tense. "Something bothering you?" he asked, but his tone did not affect Charlie the way don Pedro's had.

He laughed. "Nothing bothering me, old buddy. If you want to, though, you can do something for me."

Armando relaxed. "As I said, it's your party."

"Lend me the room for a while after my girl comes back. The same room, the same bed." He had but one thought all the time they talked to Armando. And he sat now with an enormous erection because he knew that when Shauna returned she would be a whore.

He did not see don Pedro until almost four years later in Mexico City when he was taken to him by two pistoleros. "I told you once," said the man, who was not called Pedro Villa here and who was an important official in a secretariat, "that I never give away what I own."

"What is it that I've done to you," asked Charlie, though he knew.

"You have taken one of my girls to live with you. On her it not only has not worn out, it hasn't even been broken in. She is valuable property and I have taken her back. Do this again and you will die." It was brief and the man turned back to his work. And Charlie knew he must believe him, but he was never afraid.

THIRTEEN

Driving toward the bridge, Clemente grinned suddenly. He was attracted to this man Villegas, and he knew why Lucinda had called him sexy. He thought of his people, those in America, from the militant MOCOS, as Lucinda had called them, to the Senator, another type; his own foster father, Clemente Chacón the first; and he himself—must be the third—and his wife, his mother, also dead now—definitely another type—and now this man, educated, dedicated and concerned about social progress for his people, yet different, everyone with his own goal or perhaps the goal was the same, and he thought that he, Clemente Chacón, really had the answer. He and the Senator were the only ones who understood. He remembered then that when Porfirio Díaz ran for the U.S. Senate, he and Leopoldo Smith, with Caridad, his sister (who had no business doing this because she was a Mexican citizen), and his own wife had worked with students from Austin, from UTEP, from College Station and from Houston and San Antonio; they had gone through the entire state of Texas, enfranchising Mexicans, Negroes and poor whites into a splinter group of poor people that the powerful Texas Democratic Party could not ignore, and they knew that Porfirio Díaz was serious and he convinced the bosses that he was a Democrat and a Texan and they in turn supported him. And now Porfirio Díaz was in Washington, Junior Senator from the sovereign State of Texas.

He crossed Paisano and was held up by traffic on the bridge, by pedestrians, people from Juárez who spilled onto the street, laden with bundles of used clothing and other second-hand articles. He stopped to allow a horse-drawn two-wheeled cart across the street, mildly irritated that they were still allowed on the streets of a city, and reached unconsciously under his jacket to his breast. The rent on his shirt was larger. He was at the corner and on impulse turned right, reversed his direction, sped up a one-way street free from the traffic toward his home. He would pick up a fresh shirt and his clothes for tonight. He still had many things to do this afternoon. He went up Alabama, the traffic flowing well, and he turned on his street, a bit faster than he had intended, tires screeching, but he let up before he reached his house. He saw his wife's car, and was pleasantly surprised that she was home. He bounded forward, key in hand. The blinds were drawn, and he wondered for a moment, but then went on to the door.

He glanced to the keyhole to insert the key, then straightened, and the cafe curtains on the glass were low enough to allow him to look into the living room.

"Oh, no!" he sobbed. "Oh, no, no!" as if he had just seen the body of his boy destroyed. And he leaned his head against the jamb and rocked in grief for a moment, then, in shock, he opened the door and entered. Even then they did not separate; he looked upon what he had seen through the glass. A grotesque coupling of two bodies, a scrotum old, elongated with age, wrinkled like a turkey wattle, legs and arms and movement and just as Queli looked at him with eyes distracted yet frightened over a naked shoulder, he saw distinctly three hemorrhoids protruding from Virgil Smith's anus.

The pain had left his chest and now centered somewhere above his groin, and he moved toward them, Queli now frantically pushing at Virgil and he insistent, unknowing, until she slid away from under him and on hands and knees scrambled away and into the kitchen. Virgil lay for a moment as he had been, then turned and sat, his arms behind him, supporting himself, looking at Clemente but not seeing him, and his frail body shook as quick jets of semen came from his body on the rug.

Clemente did not speak. The pain remained physical but he walked in to where his wife was. "What have you done?" he asked, and was surprised he did not shout.

She looked up at him from the stool she used when she did the cooking long ago. She smiled in hidden pleasure. He would know that what she had done was good for them. And she said, "It had to be done. You work so hard; I had to do my share for us. Now it is done." The last was in such a tone of finality that it stopped him and he looked at her, questioningly.

"Do you mean that this will never happen again if there is no need for it? Don't you see that what has just happened is important and whether it happens again or not again is not important at all?"

"You have your promotion, don't you see. Everything we ever wanted is within our reach. It is just as Virgil said, what he told me—he promised, you know."

He reached down and pulled her off the stool and slapped her hard twice, then threw her back against the counter. She slid off onto the floor and he did not help her. She stood up, still naked and said, "You do not understand or do not want to understand. I, who know everything you have done to get us here have done but a little thing to help you—to help us."

"A *little* thing! You call what you did a *little* thing? I had my promotion approved two months ago. I told you, as I tell you everything. But you could not believe me!" Again he struck her, this time beneath the ear and she slid under the counter. He knew for an excruciating moment, not devoid, somehow, of pleasure, that she felt at this point as he had felt earlier this morning when being beaten, not knowing the why of it, thinking that she had been right and now must suffer for some inexplicable reason.

Virgil Smith now stood at the entrance way, dressed as impeccably as always. His tailored suit hid the indignity of wrinkled flesh that a moment ago writhed on the floor. "You're not going to take it out on the little girl, are you, boy?"

"No," said Clemente, in a tone he would have used discussing a minor problem at the office. "No. I won't touch her again."

"For a moment I thought you would make something unpleasant out of this," said Virgil.

Now Clemente looked at him. "Unpleasant?" He uttered the word as if misunderstanding. "You polite son-of-a-bitch. You were fucking my wife and I make it unpleasant."

"It happens, you know. Some people become like animals over a simple thing like this. And I do hate scenes." Coolly, Virgil lighted a cigarette.

"I think I may yet make a scene," said Clemente in a calm voice, and his anger was clear to the other man through his calmness. "I am deciding at this moment whether or not I should kill you."

"Kill me?" Virgil shrieked the words. This had not occurred to him. "Why that's preposterous! Kill me? What are you saying? Why just this minute you said you would not strike your wife again! An irrational act for a moment, yes, I can understand that, but to kill me. You are mad!"

Clemente turned to where Queli had been cowering, but she was not there now and he had not seen her leave. "No," he said. "It is you who is insane, to think you could do a thing like this and not pay for it."

"Pay for it? Goddamn it!" And Virgil Smith in his fear was indignant. He came upon his toes and his added height was ludicrous. "I've paid! I made you what you are, what you will be tonight."

"That's bullshit!" And Clemente felt the indignity of arguing like this. "And you know it Virgil, because you don't lie. Small untruths, perhaps, but you can't lie because you believe that whatever you do is

114

right. This obscene thing you just did, even *that* you believe is right. But I have my beliefs too. Beliefs that come from way back because I'm a Mexican; you see, I cannot allow you to live."

"But it is too late," said Virgil. "We have talked too much."

"Yes, it is too late," said Clemente, as if there had been a moment when it was not too late, and he said it with sadness.

"But it is not too late," said Virgil, "to stop tonight. One phone call and it will be over for you. What will it be?"

Clemente shook his head. "You had to say it. You had to say what I know because you know what it means to me. To kill you would be meaningless. The world would be rid of nothing; you would not be hurt; I would not have the satisfaction. I could do it very easily in the next minute, but as I said, it would mean nothing. I think I've come close to making the transition—the sociologists' dream. I am very nearly devoid of cultural hang-ups. To hurt you I would have to hit you where you are vulnerable. Your position, perhaps your job is where you can be hurt most. Someday I may be able to do it."

Virgil laughed. "Forget that. You could never touch me. But I always knew I could count on you to be reasonable."

"Get out of here," said Clemente.

"I'll see you tonight," said Virgil Smith.

She sat in the living room, now fully dressed, and on her face there was no indication that anything was amiss. "Well?" she asked.

"Well what?"

"What happens now? And what about you and me?"

"It is too soon," he said. "What happens now? Well right now I'm getting a clean shirt y luego me voy al otro lado a una conferencia—oh, y también voy a ver a mi mamá." He had not thought of doing this, in fact never believed he would ever see his mother, but somehow his wife's sin had expiated his mother and he knew how much she did not want him to see his mother. At least, at this point his wife was no longer more pure than his mother. This was not thought out—he knew that until today his wife had been more pure than his mother but he also knew that at one time his mother had been as pure as his wife. He was going back across, and he knew he could not be touched by the law. And he also knew that he would now see his mother even if it meant deportation.

"Get my traje de etiqueta—I will take it along and change at the office." She rose listlessly, yet still certain that she had done nothing wrong. He was very much aware of his coldness, aware that it was over for them, even as she was aware that she could live with him for the rest of her life and it would always be like this. The coldness would dissipate, she was certain, when he realized that she, too, had done her part.

She would talk and he would not. "Listen to me, Goddamit. I'm not dumb. He told me, Mr. Smith did, that ..."

"You fucked him and call him Mr. Smith?" said Clemente and laughed. "You are incredible!"

"That is it, don't you see? He is *Mr. Smith*—not a man, not a person, but a means to get where we want to go. He may have been an obstacle. But now we are beyond him. He told me when he knew I would not go to bed with him that your prospects were good, but because you are a Mexican, you would need help. A Mexican can't get ahead in this country."

Clemente could not help believing her as she faced him, convinced that what had happened was necessary, had been destined.

"After all I have told you, you believed his bullshit? You really don't believe that someday a Mexican can be President? I think all my pain is not because you did this thing, but some of it is because you think I would approve and the major part is because you do not believe in me—in what I am capable of doing."

"I'm convinced it's true—the whites are afraid to have us get ahead."

"Jesus Christ!" Clemente was again angry. "Now you are talking colors! What is this 'white' shit? Look at yourself, look at me! We are fair-skinned and our eyes are almost blue! What would you call us, purple? If I believed in God I would say the prick is a devil—Virgil, I mean! He did a job on you and I did not even know it was happening." He paced for a moment, then pulled her to her feet. He did not kiss her, he merely held her and spoke alongside her head. "I am sorry, terribly sorry, that things have gone in the direction I did not want, did not expect. I want you to know always , that I have loved you, that I love you now and that no matter what I do, I will love you always and will remember."

"I'll see you tonight," she said, thinking that in time they would be fine again and thinking also of how much she loved him.

"I'll see you tonight," he said, repeating her statement, knowing that this was goodbye, even should he continue to live with her. For he would never forget that at the moment he entered, before she was aware of his presence, he had seen her face over Mr. Smith's skinny shoulder and it had been full of passion and pleasure, and, it seemed to him, perhaps love.

FOURTEEN

Clemente Chacón drove to Juárez through the Chamizal, near the place where Mario had sung to the beat of *don Pepe*, and into the PRONAF area looked upon by Americans as a symbol of new Mexican energy, regeneration, proof that the typical lassitude of yesterday's Mexican was truly a thing of the past. It was, in fact, a facsimile of the American shopping center, a place where the visitor from the North felt comfortable, where every clerk spoke English almost as well as the people who came to buy with the American knowledge that if it cost a great deal, it must be good.

He drove to a small branch of the Banco del Atlántico. Inside, he talked to a secretary. "I wish to see the gerente."

"Well," said the young man, "she is busy now; perhaps someone else can help you. What is your business?"

"No," he said, "I must see *her*."

"¿De parte de quién?"

"De parte de su hermano."

"I've never known her to have an older brother," said the young man.

"Please tell her I am here," said Clemente. He was suddenly very tired.

The young man walked into another office, and immediately Caridad came running and threw her arms around Clemente. "You came," she said. "You finally came to see me here!"

They were in her office and she was saying, "I've been waiting for this—I began to to think you weren't proud of me, although I knew different. All those years you paid for my education. I remember the first time Leopoldo Smith came to tell my mother that I could continue school after the secundaria. She had told him that they—she and my father—were trying to get me into one of those beauty colleges. You know Americans like to come here to get their hair done, but Leopoldo said, 'No.' I would go into a private prepa, with the monjitas, and then

117

the university." Suddenly she said, "You seem to be in pain. What is wrong with you?"

He told her about the beating; nothing about Queli.

"¡Desgraciaos...cabrones!" she exclaimed. Then, "What else is the matter? Your pain does not seem to be merely physical."

"Nothing. Except that I can't help being disillusioned that this could happen after the concern and some bit of time I have spent trying to help our youth." And he managed to laugh. But of course she was not deceived, and he knew it, so he said, "You just can't imagine the day I've had today—you don't happen to have a drink to celebrate my first visit to your bank, do you?"

"My bank!" And she laughed with him. She unlocked a cabinet. "I keep this only for very important people. *You* are most important, but I was told you did not drink."

"I don't, but I find I need one now." And he thought, how rare! I really do need one! Aloud, he said, "Who told you that?"

"Just guess."

He knew it had not been Queli, for she had not seen nor spoken to Caridad for years. He had been pained when he and Queli married, because she and his sister were friends and he felt then that he had no right to stop them from being friends, even though he wanted no ties with this side of the border. But he learned early in his marriage that his wife and his sister were not really friends. If Queli had known he was paying for his sister's education she would have objected strongly. But because he was an American only by design and he could never stop being a Mexican in some ways, he did not tell her, not as a subterfuge, but because it was not her business.

And so, he thought, it must have been Leopoldo Smith who told her that. He sipped his drink—excellent Domecq, one of the fine cognacs in the world. He said, "Very nice, your office and your company-bought liquor. I could go to sleep right here."

She said, "If you wish, there is a sofa in the anteroom." And suddenly again he was very Mexican, incongruously protective about his sister. Why would she have a bed here? And he shook his head out of the mist. It must be because he was in Mexico at this moment. He came across the border rarely.

He said, "Jesus Christ! Charity," he called her this because he had practiced and liked the sound, "I want you to take me to my mother."

Now she was serious and even angry. "No!" she said, and asked, "Why?"

"Because I need her."

"That is the only answer you could give that would make me take you to her," she said. "Although you can find her any time you wish to do so. You know, I've never judged you, never condemned you, but I don't think I can forgive you for staying away from her for so long."

"I know. A long time ago, I had to stay away to do what I set out to do. But for some years now I could have seen her and I didn't. I am so ashamed that the reason I didn't do it was because I did not approve of her past. I know that was foolish—I want to see her today and tell her this."

"You can't tell her that!" she said, changing from compassion to anger again, feeling a love for him because she knew he was good and because she sensed something was very wrong with him at this moment.

"And why not?"

"Because her husband has treated her so much like a lady and with so much love these past years, that she doesn't even remember that once she was a whore."

"Then I have sinned in a worse way than I thought," he said.

"What do you mean?" And she poured more liquor in his glass but he was unaware.

"Because that is not the reason I disapproved. I did not approve of her because she was poor. In my mind, I guess I felt she was not good enough to associate with my wife."

"Who was better than my mother? Queli? Why her mother was turning tricks on the day you were married. And her brothers were hustling the street!"

"I said that was not the reason. Understand, I was with her when she began. First to feed me, and then for the love of a man I have not forgot. I am hurting myself very much, perhaps too much for one day, but I could not afford to associate with semi-literate or illiterate campesinos if I were to achieve my meta. That was it, the poverty and the filth, not the morality of the people because I understand that, I knew that those things were survival skills. It all had to do with image. My image, and I suppose my family's image. I never thought of immorality, because it did not exist for me. I really believed that if people had what they needed, that what my mother did, what I did, would not exist. I have learned that whatever the lower classes do, the deprived, it is not immoral because it is done to survive, but when the very same things are done by the middle or upper class, it *is* immoral, because it is done for pleasure. There is no need for it. I made one mistake, because I did not read. I have been so involved in the idea of upward mobility, that I do not know what it is. And please do not forget that I, too, hustled the street."

"But this is different. Calixta's mother sent them out to hustle and to pimp. Your mother—my mother—sent you out to do clean and honest work. She spent her last few cents to buy you a shoeshine kit because she felt you would work for your money. And she only wavered once, when she sent me to you. But she always grieved for you and worried about you, and as far as we were concerned, I and the rest of the children, you were her only child. Oh, she did not neglect us, did not mistreat us, but she did not let us forget it. And we hated you without knowing you. I hated you too, but when I saw you that day, I loved you. I love you now, not because you sent me to school, but because I realized that you loved her, because I recognized your compassion.

"But this is too much talk because I should not chastise you. And I shall take you to her, because it is proper that I should do so."

"We *must* talk," he said. "There is more you must know. I remember Cipriano, he whom you call 'father.' Cipriano, el panzón, we called him on the street. He drove his hack I think twenty-four hours a day. He would slide himself under the steering wheel, barely fitting his belly under it and roar off with a fare. But even before that, in Mexico, I was very young, but I clearly remember when we arrived there. And I remember everything since then, but I remember very little before that. Our village, actually it was but a small colonia, not even a village; I know mostly what I was told about it. But in Mexico I remember everything. I remember when the first man came, and I remember what my mother and I were to each other. How truly beautiful she was."

"She still is beautiful," said Caridad.

"Yes, she must be," he said, "because you are. Yes, I remember the first man—a man who came into our lives, and I have never been able to forget him. A Gringo, as you people say. He brought us here, and then he died. And that is the first time I saw Cipriano. He would park his cab near the place where my mother worked. He always looked out for her, and all the other people on the street laughed at him. She was bad then. She was very bad after the other died. She drank all the time and she smoked. It was terrible for me in a little room where we lived, so I began to sleep on the street with the other boys whose mothers worked like mine. Then one day she was thrown out of the cantina where she worked. She was of no further use to them—they would not let her go before that, don't you see? I knew it would turn out like this, I had seen it, but I did not expect it now. And that night, when they were finished with her, she came out of the place like a shot, and the other whores were laughing at her, not knowing they faced the same fate. All this was told to me later by people who saw it. And I was told that as she lay senseless against a wall, before the chotas came, Cipriano picked her up and took her to his rooms. He undressed her and put her in bed, then he went out and found me. He arranged a petate for me near the bed, then he went away to work. 'Do not leave this place,' he said to me. 'Your mother is very sick.' Then he went away.

"We were there like this for over a month. Every day Cipriano brought food, and at first he would fix it for us. Later my mother was alright, but she was always sad. I expected all along that Cipriano would come home and lie with my mother—I knew about those things—but he never did. If he slept at all, he slept in his cab. I knew he was a good person, but I hated him, resented him. I suppose I resented him as much for myself as for the other one. The one who died. Christ! I have so much to atone for."

She was moved, in her mind seeing Clemente as a little boy, suffering not only hunger, but the stigma that his mother gave him and the ostracism because of that fact. She said, "You still haven't told me what is wrong."

He did not answer.

"It *is* Calixta, is it not?"

"Yes, it is something between Queli and me, but I will not discuss it."

She nodded. It has to be her doing, she decided. Already she was mentally loyal to her brother, who had now returned.

"When are you going to Mexico?" he asked.

"I'm not."

"Oh?" he was surprised. "You told me it was all set."

"It is set," she said, "but I turned it down. I'm going to keep this job for a while."

"I'm glad," he said, "I know it's much better for you, professionally, to go down there, but now that I will be seeing you more often, I'm selfishly thinking I want you here."

She smiled, and now she, too, was drinking. "You know, the only reason I regret not going is because I'm giving up a chance to do so much for Mexican womanhood. Don't laugh! I know what life is for women on this side. The very things you told me about our own mother. And this company is good about it. They don't pay much, of course, but half of their small branches like this one are managed by women. They offered me a sucursal in Lomas de Chapultepec because I speak English. And it is a good, prestige position because everyone in that area is rich. In a few years I could have an assistantship in a large branch, maybe even a position in the matrix, but I'm going to be married and I must be with my husband."

"Married! Who is he? What does he do?"

She laughed. "Really, Clemente, you are rare, and you are raza. You've returned only a few minutes ago and already you are planning to disapprove of my choice for a husband. You're so stern and straight, I bet you've never been with another woman since your marriage."

"I have never been with a women other than my wife, even before I married," he said almost primly. "But who is this fellow? What does he do?" He would not be sidetracked.

"You're priceless," she said, now more American than he had ever been. "Even after the life you have led, the things you have done to get where you are, you were never with a woman!"

"You forget I grew up in whorehouses. I loved these women, my mother's friends, and I can never abuse them. I have been exposed to everything, and that is why I've kept away from everything, including drink. I don't drink except for a moment like this and I have not had such moments. I sold mota and I have never smoked, I sold women and I have never used one. I have seen the end result of these things; every day someone is at the end of the road and I simply have kept away from them. But I shouldn't talk to you like this..."

"There you go again."

"I think I'm beginning to feel all this drink."

"You've only had two."

But he was not listening. "Once," he said, "when I was selling knives and forks—I was about seventeen, I guess—there was a Gringa," she laughed because he was speaking like a Mexican now, "with whom I was madly in love. She must not have been more than thirty. I always stopped at her home late in the afternoon on my way home because she would always buy one place setting. I knew why she bought them, and I suppose I went there late because I knew her husband would soon be home. I knew that much, but one day I decided I might as well find out what it was all about. I went there at ten o'clock in the morning, and when she opened the door, she was stark-naked and she didn't say a word, but took me by the hand and led me into a bedroom. Suddenly I, who had never had a headache in my life, had a headache. Not a plain old headache, but the grandfather of all headaches. I could barely see, and of course, I did nothing."

"Did she buy more knives and forks?"

"No."

"You are a lousy salesman."

He looked at her, wondering how she knew. "Who is this guy?" again he asked.

This time she did not laugh. She gave him some more to drink, pouring very deliberately, then she said, "Leopoldo Smith. You should have known." She watched him very carefully, wishing with all her heart that he would not disapprove, thinking that all along she wanted his blessing.

He grinned, and he showed his surprise. "Well, I'm not unhappy it is Leopoldo. But how did this happen? And why should I have known, and why didn't I?"

"Why would you have known? You haven't been on this side for some time. But it was because of you that I saw so much of him, and that is not completely true, I must admit. The last two years we have been seeing each other because we wished to do so, by design. Actually, the last year I was at the University, he came to see me more than usual. From the first, when he found a family where I could live and took me to Chihuahua, he looked out for me. He would come at least once a month, and sometimes he would talk to my teachers, and he always looked over my grades. Once, I asked him why he did this and he said because you were his friend and he had been on the street with you and I did not understand and in my last year I knew I loved him and really believed there was someone else because I was treated like a little sister. And when I came home and began to work at the bank, we saw each other quite a bit and suddenly two weeks ago he asked me to marry him. You can't imagine how happy I am!"

"Yes, I can," he said. "Today, especially, I can clearly remember how happy I was when Calixta said she would be my wife." Despite his resolve, his face fell, his voice wavered.

"You still won't talk about it?"

He shook his head. And he recovered from his momentary lapse and said, "I'm very happy for you—for both of you I'm very happy. Leopoldo has always been a good friend; he has been more than a friend as you well know, and strangely, we have never really been intimates." He thought of Leopoldo from way back, when the boy, who was older than he and Mario, slopped floors and cleaned out toilets. And later, when Leopoldo turned his business over to him, Clemente had realized that he and Leopoldo were the only two left of those who worked the street who had always known what they wanted. The other, Mario, was, of course, dead. "I have to talk to Leopoldo," he said. "Call him for me will you?"

"Are you going to tell him not to beat me when we are married, and will you also tell him that he should not have mistresses like all Mexican men do?" she said, and she laughed.

Clemente did not laugh. "He won't beat you because he loves you." He thought strongly of his wife, whom he had struck. "And as for mistresses, it is up to you to see that he does not need one." Again his mood seemed to change, but he brought himself out of it with a physical effort, and yet he wondered why he suddenly thought of this possibility for him. That he might now take a woman. He was nervous, almost as if he was at this moment being unfaithful, as if right now he had to decide whether to take a mistress. As if everything would be right; so that everything would be balanced, to do what she had done might make their marriage what it had been. "Actually," he said, "I was to have gone to a meeting with him."

"I know. He told me."

"I'm not going to that meeting after all, and I must let him know so he can notify the others. I'm not going to see my mother either."

She showed her disappointment. "Why not? Why?" she asked. "You had convinced me that you wanted to see her! That you had returned to us!"

"Wait a minute." He raised his hand. "There is simply not enough time for me to do the things I must do today. I don't want to stop by for a few minutes. I want to spend some time with her. I'll be back from the East in a week. I will come then but not like a hurt little boy. And I'll bring her something."

"You don't have to bring her anything. You know that." But she was happy.

"I'm bringing little Pete," he said.

Now she was radiant. "She'll like that. Oh, how she'll like that. Her first grandchild! May I tell her?"

"Of course, if you wish. Anyway, from now on he'll spend time here. I will let him stay with her a week or two at a time if she'll have him. He has to know where he comes from; he has to learn some Spanish. And he won't begin to think he's better than a Mexican when he learns he is really one himself."

"Is that what they teach them over there on the other side?"

"That's what some people teach them."

She stared in disbelief. Not only because she knew he was referring to his wife, but because she was truly confused. "I don't understand you," she said. "What *do* you want him to be, Mexican or American?"

"I don't understand it either. But I don't want him to forget that he's a Mexican."

"Because you've decided you're a Mexican?"

"Because I've never stopped being Mexican. I know I never will, no matter what I become. I am a Mexican and I am an American, and there is no reason in the world why I can't be both."

He did not speak for a time. She sat looking at him, smiling a secret, wistful smile, and finally she said, "Leopoldo will be here soon. He was to drop me off at home before your meeting."

"Let's have one more drink, then," he said. "Thinking of what I just said, Leopoldo is a case in point. What is Leopoldo? A Mexican. Even if he has Negro blood, he is a Mexican. He would never deny his Negro background to feel that he is Mexican. It isn't because he believes the Negro is inferior, as some of our people do, that he will say he is a Mexican. Very simply, he is a Mexican. You know of his black blood, of course."

"Now wait a minute!" She was very angry. "Just what are you trying to do? Do you believe that would make a difference to me?"

He did not react to her anger. "I didn't think about it at all until this minute. Now it is important to me to know whether it matters to you. For Leopoldo's sake, not for yours."

"Why? Does it make a difference to you?"

"Jesus Christ, no! But if you should have even the least apprehension about it, then it would be a terrible thing to marry him. That is all, and for that reason I'm concerned. I'm sorry if it was not clear. But it is because we don't hide these things ... "

"*We*, the Mexican you or the American you?"

"You didn't let me finish. I mean that in the United States a drop of black blood is considered offensive, so it is hidden. Perfectly good people, Christian, democratic people who have no prejudices of their own are frightened into acting in this way. Some who have more than a little of the blood will pass as white if they are fair enough, while others who are as dark as our people will live a lie thinking they have the world fooled."

She said, "For a while I thought you had been on the other side too long. That perhaps you'd picked up some of our people's paranoia over there—Goddamn Chicanos, they claim they hate the Gringo and they imitate him even down to his latest prejudices. They accuse him of racism and become racists themselves! Jesus!"

Her phone buzzed. "Ya llegó el licenciado Smith," said her secretary.

"Que pase," said Caridad.

Leopoldo Smith walked in. Slim, tall, with his clothes hanging on him as if he had been created to their specifications.

"Clemente," he said with obvious pleasure. "¿Qué dices, hombre? ¡Qué milagro!"

"Aquí nomás, Leopoldo," said Clemente as they embraced.

"I talk to you every week," said Leopoldo, "but it has been weeks since I've seen you."

"Busy," said Clemente.

Happily, possessively watching them, Caridad said, "You may kiss me, Polo. He knows."

Leopoldo was serious. He looked at Clemente and said, "¿Y?"

"¿Quién lo hubiera pensado, cabrón? Pero estoy encantado. Felicidades a los dos." He laughed at Leopoldo. "But look, man," he said, "this is the twentieth century—you seem nervous, as if you need the approval of the brother of the bride."

"You're right," said Leopoldo. "I am nervous, and it is important because Caridad wants your approval, and because I love you." He raised a hand. "Wait," he said, anticipating Clemente's question. "Because you are the man you are, because of what you have done for Cari, then because you are a part of my past as I am a part of yours. You know, we've done pretty much what we set out to do, and on our own terms. I remember the old times, and I think if you or I had ever told anyone our dreams then, they would have called us crazy, because our vision was impossible."

"I understand," said Clemente. "And it seems so long ago but it really isn't, because I have something for you that will bring us back. You told me three or four telephone calls ago that Mario's mother lived. I always believed she was dead—he told me so."

"He told you that because he was more ashamed than we about our mothers being whores."

So he did have a weakness, Clemente thought, but he did not say it aloud. Yet, he was not overjoyed as he once thought he would be if he could find it. Mario, who always taught him that he should never forget that he was number one. Tell them nothing—you are number one, even though I may someday fuck you out of everything you have, it would not have happened if you really believed you were number one, Mario had once said to him. Now aloud, he said, "Anyway, he is dead and I took this from his clothes when he died." He reached into an inside pocket.

"Dead?" asked Leopoldo, surprised and frightened, because long ago, Mario was indestructible. "I always believed," he said, "that Mario merely went away somewhere until it came time for him to be President of the Republic."

"He died," said Clemente, handing Leopoldo the passbook. "I don't know why I took it, but I know why I've kept it all these years. I know that wherever he is, if he is, he is disappointed in me, because if the situation were reversed, he would have found a way to get to the money. It isn't much—a couple of thousand pesos sixteen years ago—but try to get it to his mother." He looked at Leopoldo, amazed that he, too, had been under Mario's spell.

Leopoldo said, "I can take care of that end of it. The difficult part is to convince her that he is dead. Are you certain?"

"He drowned," said Clemente. "We were alone in the canal when he died. I don't want to do it, but if it is necessary, I'll tell her how he died."

"I'll take care of it," said Leopoldo. He took the bank book and put it in his pocket. Caridad was alongside him, her arm around his waist.

"Yo también te pido un favor," she said.

"Lo que sea."

"The chicken noses beat Clemente this morning. I want someone hurt."

"Chicken noses?" asked Clemente.

"That's what we call them on this side, those of us who speak English. Chicanos—*Chicken nose*—you get it?"

"They would not think it very funny," said Clemente.

"I don't think what they did to you is funny, either," she answered. Leopoldo looked terrifying in his anger. "Who?" he asked.

Clemente shrugged his shoulders. "There were three of them. I have never seen them before today."

"Where?" asked Leopoldo.

"In my office, this morning around 8:30, I guess."

"What did they look like?"

"One was chaparro y flaco. Con un bigotito. Hatchet face. Another looked like Benito Juárez, only larger. I don't remember the third one too well."

Leopoldo was very quiet. He picked up the phone and dialed.

"I don't want you to do anything about it," said Clemente. "Let it pass."

"I can't let it pass," said Leopoldo. "When they get on you, they're fucking around with me and they must understand that they can't get away with these things. Bueno," he said into the mouthpiece. "Déjeme hablar con Lázaro López."

"Goddamn it, no!" shouted Clemente. "That man's a killer, for Christ Sake! Is that how you propose to make them understand?"

Leopoldo waved an arm to quiet him, almost as if he had not understood his words. "Pinche Lázaro," he said. "Tiene su familia en El

127

Diablo y su casa chica aquí, y nunca sabe uno dónde se encuentra." He dialed another number. "Habla Leopoldo Smith," he said. "Three of your paisanos did a job on one of my brothers this morning... All I know is that there were three of them, one of them was an Indian ... no pendejo, one of our kind of Indians, como tú. They were university students, in the movement, militant. They hit him in his office between eight and nine this morning... no, he doesn't want that and I don't either, but I'm well pissed about it. I want to know who they are, who their friends are, their parents, and what they do for a living outside of going to school on a free ride. I want to know that especially, although once I know who they are I can find out. And I want to talk to them personally." He hung up and slowly turned to Clemente. "How do you know he's a killer?" he asked.

"I didn't know you still did business with those people," said Clemente, showing his disgust.

"Only legal business," said Leopoldo, "and only honest business. Their dirty work is done by lawyers I don't even speak with. They have legitimate business interests on the other side—don't forget I spent a year at Harvard studying international law so that I could work both sides of the river. But you did not answer my question. Do *you* still work for them?"

Clemente was angry. "Work for *them*! You should know better than that. I did once... you recruited me, remember? But I didn't know then that they were responsible for things that happened in my life. I was very young, and very, very dumb. I know he's a killer because I saw him kill..."

"He can never know this," said Leopoldo.

"I was five or six years old at the time," said Clemente. "What harm can I do him now?"

"Nevertheless, he musn't know," said Leopoldo.

Clemente shrugged. It really did not matter to him now. "I learned years later that the man he killed had been his best friend. Perhaps the only friend he ever had or will have. I saw him once after that, just before I stopped working for them. He came into the grocery store and said, 'I'm Lázaro López. I'm here to pick up.' All those years, and suddenly there he was talking to me. But he had not really seen me the first time, perhaps for a minute when he took us to the car at the train station and when they took my mother and me to a small room above a cantina. But I could not forget him, and I'm surprised that I never saw him on the street. He must have been there. And this day, suddenly I knew who my bosses were. The same people who owned my mother in

Mexico and later owned her here in Juárez. I knew that I was finished with that, even before el Pingüino and Chito killed that other poor bastard, but now Lázaro López was waiting for the money. And although I knew it was alright to give it to him, I said, 'I don't know what you're talking about man. Pick up what?' and he looked at me for a long time, and oddly I wasn't afraid, and finally he grinned and said, 'I think they'll like that. They'll think you're pretty smart—the regular guy will be by next week. This isn't my line of work anyway.' He left, and had no idea I knew about his line of work.

"And that's how I know he's a killer. I don't want his help."

"He won't even see those people," said Leopoldo. "But he will get me the information I need. Don't worry about them or him."

"I'm not worried," said Clemente. And he changed the line of talk. "I'm not going to that meeting after all. Explain it to them, will you?"

"Your mind is made up?"

"My mind has been made up, as I told you so many times, yet there was always a small chance that I would not come with you. Today I almost decided not to do it, but now I know just where I am going and how I'm going to get there. I'll be on the border a year, maybe two. Then I'm going to Los Angeles. Before too long, the Company will give me pretty much what I want."

Caridad was surprised and showed it. "Does Queli like the idea of going so far away?" she asked.

"She isn't in my plans," said Clemente.

Now Leopoldo was surprised and for a moment quiet, then knowing that Clemente would not talk about it, he asked, "Are you still inclined to put some capital into the project?"

"I gave my word on that, why do you ask?"

"Because things are changed now," said Leopoldo. "I expected that you would watch over our investment, but now I'll have to do it, at least for a while. But you and I must come up with more money. The loan is set—twelve million pesos when the firm deposits two million, but now our partners won't be able to secure the loan unless they can come up with another half million."

"Why is that?" asked Clemente.

"Because now only three persons will be Mexican citizens and by law, foreign interest can be only 49 percent. You see, I'm jumping the line, too. I'm picking up my American citizenship."

Caridad gasped. "Why haven't you told me?" she asked.

"I came here to tell you," said Leopoldo, and seemed somehow excited. "The Senator woke me up this morning and talked to me until I

129

agreed to work with him. You know he has been after me for a long time—I always refused but he made it sound quite interesting. So, in about a year, we will be in Washington."

Clemente watched to see how his sister reacted to this news. He, too, had made an important decision a few minutes ago, but he did not have to share the knowledge with anyone. Not yet, at least. He was happy to see Caridad simply put her arms around Leopoldo and wondered how long she would remain a Mexican woman.

"That is why," said Leopoldo, speaking over Caridad's shoulder, "we have to come up with another half million. That means forty thousand dollars apiece instead of twenty, but we will own forty percent of the business between us. Can you do it?"

"How are you going to keep an eye on things?"

"For the first year I'll be active in it. After that, I'll be on permanent retainer, heading the legal staff, checking in every couple of months or so. The Company's lawyers will be my people. My role, since I can practice in Mexico, will be explicit in the incorporation papers."

"Alright," said Clemente. "You know how I feel about insurance. There is no way we can lose. I wish I could take a part in it at this end, but I can't. To make a company grow, my own company or at least as much mine as it will be my partners! That would be something! But it can't be for me because it can only be done in Mexico. I could never have the capital to do it in my country, could never have enough even to get into something like this. I may be able to swing it without having to borrow. I'm selling everything. The house, my car, a couple of building lots where I was to have built Queli her home."

Caridad said, "I won't say anything more about your wife, although you keep dropping hints. But what is this hatred you seem to have for Mexico?"

Clemente was genuinely surprised. He was so certain in his mind why he must continue to work and live as an American that he believed every one could understand. "I'm sorry you believe that," he said. "I don't hate Mexico, although I do hate the life I led there. Yet, it taught me there could be something better, it prepared me for what I must do with my life. Perhaps it even taught me the value of life. And someday, I will return to Mexico. When I am finished with my work, I may find me a place in the mountains of Michoacán or on the coast and there live out my time." He said to Leopoldo, "About the stock in the new company, I want half to be in Queli's name, OK? And I want you to draw up papers so that it will go to little Pete when she dies."

"OK, mano," said Leopoldo. "But there is another little matter I should discuss with you now. You have some property in Mexico. About three hundred acres—all legal. Your actual father left it to you. There is nothing on it, mostly it is prairie, but it has some of the richest soil in Mexico. Your mother has paid the taxes on it, and I had it fenced. I also arranged for a sharecropper to work about forty acres so that the government would not take it away from you. He built a one room jacal, but that is the only building."

"I don't want it," said Clemente.

"You're not only being foolish, but childish," said Leopoldo. He would not disguise his anger.

Clemente was also angry. "Just what in hell are all you people doing minding my business and not even telling me? Christ, you think me a child!"

"Goddamn it, you're acting like one!"

"You've been down there?" asked Clemente, his anger over.

"To Zacatecas? Yes. Your grandfather is dead—shot in a cantina, but your greatgrandfather still lives."

"I remember him. I really do remember him," said Clemente in surprise.

"You want me to sell the land?"

"No. Let's hang on to it."

FIFTEEN

Clemente Chacón sat at his desk more relaxed than he had been at any time this day. Lucinda brushed and hung his clothes in the closet. She emerged from the small room smiling.

"I don't know what brand it was, Clem, but you should try it more often. You look mighty happy sitting there."

"I guess I should," he said, grinning. "Let's have some coffee, you and I, and bring your telephone numbers with you."

When she returned with the coffee and her book, he was standing at the window, with his hands behind his back, looking down into the parking lot. He closed the door before he sat down again. "I want you to get Max Calhoun on the line," he said. "but I don't want Ruth Knickrem or Virgil to know about this call."

She did not look at him, did not question although this was unusual. She reached Calhoun on her third attempt.

"Max," he said. "This is Clemente Chacón. Is Virgil with you? ... Good! Listen, I want to talk to you alone, to discuss something with you that will be of mutual benefit. Yes, alone ... no, of course I can't talk on the telephone. Where are you? OK. There's a small bar a few blocks from where you are. The Nooner. It's across from the main post office. Just tell the cab driver, he'll know ... in a half hour."

He thought for a minute. Then he looked at Lucinda and said, "I'm sorry I can't tell you what I'm doing yet. I will later, but can't at this moment."

She nodded.

"One thing I can tell you, though," he said. "I'm taking a big chance, and I very stupidly left myself unprotected. Please try Leopoldo Smith's office. They may know where he can be reached. When I left him he was on his way to take my sister home."

"I have Caridad's home number," she said.

"How?" he asked. "Why?" And he was surprised.

"Because I am an efficient secretary. I wanted it in case you should someday need it. Now your sister and I have become friends—she calls now and then to see how you are, and we sometimes meet for lunch." She was dialing. "She and Leopoldo have been to my place."

Again he was surprised, but he knew that was not his concern. "They are going to be married," he said.

She placed the receiver down. "And you—how do you feel about that?" she asked.

"I feel very good about it," he said. "Why? Shouldn't I feel happy? And why do you question me?"

"Forgive me," she said. "I should not question you. I have become very fond of your sister and I suppose I came to share her apprehendions. I got the impression from Caridad that if she should marry Leopoldo you might disapprove."

She dialed again.

He would have spoken, but he was suddenly angry, thinking again that many things were happening behind his back, and it seemed that his sister and Lucinda had deliberately hidden their friendship from him.

Soon she said, "Caridad? Lucinda," and she pronounced her name as if it were Spanish. "Felicidades," she said, "acaba de decírmelo tu hermano...No. I'll see you tonight. Clem wants to talk to you." She handed him the telephone, and he was looking at her in amazement. He knew that she had picked up a word or two in Spanish, a phrase, perhaps, but living on the border she could not help learning a little.

She had not told him she had been studying, that she had Mexican friends with whom she practiced, nor did he know that she, too, had a tape recorder. And he did not know, also, that she had met his mother.

He did not say hello, he simply asked, "Did Leopoldo leave for the meeting? Tell him, then, that I don't want him to say anything yet. Tell them to wait until I talk with him tonight. No. I'm still in, only I may yet come home to stay. A few hours. I'll explain when I see him tonight."

When he hung up, there was no doubt that he was relieved. He smiled at Lucinda. "I think everything is OK now," he said. "But for a minute there, I may have made the biggest mistake of my life." He studied her a moment. "How about another cup of coffee?"

"Not for me," she said, getting up, "but I'll bring you some."

"Never mind," he said. He rose and walked to the window, then paced across the room. She waited, for she knew she was not dismissed, thinking he was deciding to tell her what he was up to. But he surprised her.

"About tonight," he said. "I'll come, but I want to be alone with you. Will your guests be gone by midnight?"

133

"They will if I ask them to leave." She did not show her feelings, though she understood what he meant. And she did not think of what they would be doing to Queli. She had made up her mind about this long ago, and Queli did not concern her.

"What will you tell them?"

"I'll simply say that I'm expecting a man."

He looked at her and wondered. Again she knew what he was thinking, and she smiled and said, "This is a different age, Mr. Chacón. These things can be said among friends," but now she sensed that something was very wrong, and she grasped his arm strongly, even as he said:

"Then you have been candid with them at other times?"

She turned him toward her and looked into his face and said, "No, Clem. You are the first one, the very first. Since my marriage broke up I have not been with a man. In fact, the only man I have ever known was my husband, and he wasn't really a man. And now you are coming tonight to fuck with me—I must have it that way, you see, even though I may shock you—you fuck with me, you do not fuck me. I want it, I have been wanting this for a long time, and I think I may finally know what it is all about with you. I know that I do, but are you certain you want to do this?"

He was a fool, he knew, for feeling the way he did. What she did was her business. And so to cover up his pain, he said, mock-seriously, "Of course I'm sure, Miss Gray. Did you ever know me to do a thing when I wasn't sure?"

She touched his lips lightly with her fingertips and said only, "I'll be alone at one." And she walked away from him.

He had wondered why he wanted to do this, when he finally decided to do it. It must have been when his sister told him she would marry. He was not certain, but he had been troubled by the idea that his behavior was caused by a desire to hurt Queli. And he thought also, that this might mean he would live his life now in that pattern practiced by his acquaintances that he detested so much. On the town two or three times a week, hopping from bed to bed. He knew now that one of the reasons for beginning a relationship with Lucinda was that it must be a lasting thing. And now feeling a jealousy he seemed unable to control, he recognized he had made a total commitment. He and Queli were through, he also knew. Despite his efforts to make a transition into the world of the Anglo American, he had failed, for his Mexican side would never allow him to restore Queli to her place as his wife. He knew the torture he would suffer if he remained with her, knew for certain that the scene, the hideous scene of coupled bodies would haunt him forever. He loved her. He forgave her. But to live with her meant his destruction. As for Lucinda, would he now become with her what he had never been? A jealous, suspicious man, half-crazed with fear that she, too, might betray him?

Max Calhoun held a glass of scotch in his large hand as Clemente joined him in the booth of the dimly lighted cocktail lounge. He casually waved an arm to call the waitress.

"What are you drinking, Clem?"

"Brandy—straight. I'm not a drinker, Max."

"I know. At the home office they think you don't drink at all."

Clemente laughed. "That's almost true," he said. He had his drink now. "Once in a great while I'll have a couple. Today I've had about eight, but then, this is a very special day."

Calhoun watched him carefully, then drank half his drink and said, "OK, let's cut the polite shit. I want to know what you have to say, but first let me tell you this. I don't like to be jacked the way you did me with Virgil this morning. But I'm a Company man. That's why I've never been with an agency. I've got to be a part of what I sell. You're an asset to the Company, so I'm for you. I don't hold grudges against people who are good for the firm. So I checked your new man out—Villegas. He's the real goods. He's been everywhere, it seems, and wherever he's been they say the same thing. He's first rate, except for one thing. He isn't steady."

"What do you mean? Is he a drunk or something?"

"Well, no," said Calhoun. "He works for you, and he does his work. And he's there on time every day and every night if necessary. Only he's a little goofy. He only lasts a year or so, then one day he says, 'I've had it for this job,' and gives notice. The son of a bitch could be working on Madison Avenue! One guy I know pretty well personally and professionally was going to promote him, healthy increase, more vacation time, and when he told him, your man quit. 'Make it too attractive for me here and I'm trapped,' he said. One year, two at the most. That's all the time you have him. Crazy bastard wants to sit around writing monographs, or whatever the fuck they call them. No money in it, but you might as well get used to the idea."

"That's fine," said Clemente. "That's about how long I need him."

"Now what did you want to talk about?"

"I caught Virgil fucking my wife today," said Clemente as easily as if they were making small talk.

Calhoun stared, momentarily speechless. His jaw hung slack, and finally he spoke. "You're the most cold-blooded bastard I've ever known," he said.

Clemente was thinking, *not cold-blooded. Not cold-blooded at all, Max. You can't see what is happening inside me at this moment.* For in uttering the words in that manner, he relived the scene, he experienced again the death blow he had suffered, and he could bear it only because he knew it would be the last time.

"And smart, too," said Calhoun. "I never realized how much smarts you have. Like the way you handled me this morning. How'd you learn these things in this stinking border town?"

"The border is a jungle," said Clemente. "Instincts develop early here. But I'm not really cold-blooded as you called me, although you can call me ruthless in business."

"Everywhere is a jungle," said Calhoun. "What do you expect me to do?"

Clemente laughed aloud. "You're the one who said we should cut out the polite shit. You know what I want."

Calhoun called for more drinks, and they were both silent. The fact that the other must think gave Clemente confidence. Although he had met him only once, he knew about Mr. Smith in Connecticut—Chairman of the Board. He did know the younger brother, President of the Company. Descendants of Puritans and puritannical, they forgave nothing that would taint the good name of the Company. They had always tolerated Virgil's affairs, because his discretion was of the highest order. With the Company, it really did not matter what the employee did. It was not "why did you do it?" but "why did you allow yourself to be found out?" And the Company would not tolerate this of today if they knew. It was in Calhoun's power to decide whether they should know. They had people like him to cushion them and keep their moral code from damaging the Company their great-great-granddaddy had founded. There was only one fear in Clemente's mind, and that was how much Virgil was still worth to the Company. In the final analysis, really, it came to Calhoun's decision as to which of the two, Clemente or Virgil, was expendable.

This time Calhoun drained his glass and again waved an arm. "Like I said," he began, "you're smart. And you *are* a merciless son of a bitch to use your wife in this way."

"*He* used her," said Clemente, and the other did not know how angry Clemente was.

"Alright," said Calhoun. "You're a salesman; sell yourself."

Clemente thought, *you're smart, too, you bastard*, because Calhoun was forcing him to tell him what he wanted. Forcing him to somehow stand naked by stating that he wanted Virgil fired so that he would not stand in his way. "You know it isn't true," said Clemente. "I don't have to sell myself. You know my record, you know my growth potential, my capabilities, my worth to the Company. You want me to build a case against Virgil. I think I can. Aside from today, he's been banging his secretary for some time. A cardinal sin for Company executives. Of course that's not important in your decision. Just a little extra if you make your report. What is important is that Virgil has reached his level. One more step upward will place him beyond his ability. Here, because he has someone like me, directly under him, he has done a great job. When he goes to Los Angeles, people like me will be hundreds, maybe a thousand miles away from his base. And we will have others under us doing the real work. Virgil can make decisions on the spot, but he doesn't have the imagination necessary for a broad operation. Oh, his experience will carry him through, but at best he will only be adequate. The Company will not suffer if he goes to Los Angeles, but it also will not suffer if he doesn't. That's the case."

"And you," said Calhoun. "You think you can do the Los Angeles job?"

"I can do it now, perhaps better than anyone else in the Company, but I think I must prove myself in this new position before the East would consider such a move. A year, two at the most, and I'll be moving up. If not the coast, somewhere else."

"What you say about Virgil is true," said Calhoun. "You know it, I know it, but what if the Company doesn't know it?"

"I think the Company does."

"Why?"

"Because you wouldn't know it if it didn't. And because he has not been moved East. He's always said he is out here because he wants to be where the action is. And that he would never accept an appointment at the home office where he would wither on the vine, as he puts it. But I know Virgil—he can be pompous and he likes to feel important. He would love the idea of being in the East, especially since being there might get him on the Board someday."

"You may be right," said Calhoun, "but not entirely. One reason he's out here is that he has always done a tremendous job with young people like you. I don't have to tell you how much he's taught you. And he was in the home office some years back, but was shipped out for doing to a junior member what he did to you today. The kid didn't stand a chance, though. He wasn't in your position and even if he had been, maybe he didn't have the calculating ambitions you have. Took a couple thousand dollars to keep him from bringing an alienation of affection suit against Virgil, although I don't think he was really going to do it. And Virgil was shipped out to the sticks where he could continue to do the great job he could do, which is what had got him to the home office in the first place. Smith and Smith knew about it, of course, but not officially. Decisions for official reports are made by people like me."

He had won, yet curiously Clemente felt no elation, no sense of relief.

Calhoun ran a hand over his face. "These things are never pleasant, you know. It isn't easy to decide to kick out a thirty-year employee who has always contributed to the Company. At least Virgil won't be hurting. He was to be a vice president in L.A.—loss of that will hurt his ego. But maybe they'll give him the title anyway before they lower the boom, because there will be nothing unpleasant in his departure. He will be retired gracefully. He'll get a full pension and he has stock in the Company." He now looked up at Clemente. "Another drink?" he asked.

"No. I've had enough."

"Well, I better get back to my hotel. I've got a phone call to make. You had better cancel your trip for now. I'm certain one of the Smiths, maybe both of them, will be here tomorrow, the day after at the latest. I must tell you that there's a chance, an outside chance that you'll get Los Angeles inside three months. We have a guy there, a Chicano, quite a bit older than you, who can handle this job. I'm going to recommend that he be brought out here until you can turn everything over to him. I'm also going to recommend that you get the L.A. job—Virgil's job. That's what you wanted all along, isn't it?"

Clemente did not answer. "Keep talking," he said.

"And Virgil will also recommend you."

"Virgil? Why would he do that?" Clemente suddenly had trouble breathing.

"Because Virgil will do what is best for the Company. We're conditioned to be this way. And that's what I like about family companies. You're conditioned also, but only to a point. You know I hate Virgil, the little prick, but I'm not pulling the string on him because of that. I'm doing it in the best interest of the Company and I'm recommending you for the same reason. I know what you can do. I'm taking a chance because you think more of Clemente Chacón and his ambitions than the Company."

Again Clemente did not comment on Calhoun's statements. "There is one more thing," he said. "I'm going to divorce my wife."

"Do you have to? Simply for an indiscretion? Can't you talk it out and put it together again?"

"No. I must leave her."

"Have you been thinking about this for some time?"

"I have never thought about it. I am not thinking about it now. I simply know I must do it."

"Talk to Mr. Smith, then. He won't allow you to use the grounds of adultery in court, but yours is the only situation where they condone divorce."

"It will be done in Mexico," said Clemente. "I'm taking rooms there for residency purposes." Then he decided to talk to Calhoun. "One more thing and this is the last," he said. "I don't know why but I want you to understand this. I didn't tell you about today for the reasons you think. To tell you what I did was the most difficult thing I've ever had to do. Because revealing it to others makes me as common, as vulgar as people who do such things. I have never thought of the possibility of this happening to me, because such a thing simply could not. I now know different. You say I told you to further my ambitions. You're wrong. You say I have no company loyalty; you are wrong again. I am reacting to a terrible harm that was done to me. I, Clemente Chacón, hurt, not the Company. Oh, I knew that if Virgil went, I could eventually benefit, but I did it to hurt him where it would hurt him most. This is the only way I can get back at him, and I find I must have some form of revenge. I always believed that when I achieved success I would rise above old customs and traditions. I very nearly have, but obviously not enough. You're not a Mexican, so you can't even begin to understand. I can't even comprehend it fully. I only know that the old culture still has a stranglehold on me."

"And what if you had failed?" asked Calhoun.

"But I didn't," said Clemente.

Now that Calhoun had gone, Clemente suddenly wanted more to drink. He called the waitress and switched to scotch. He thought of his wife and how in a few moments their lives had changed. Back through the years, remembering, wondering if perhaps things had not really begun to change back there somewhere. And he could not remember. Sex, yes, it had been a problem between them. He had been unsatisfied, but only he knew this, and he had explained the situation to himself by simply accepting the fact that her sexual appetite had diminished. And now this? Again he must believe that she had betrayed him thinking she was helping him—that it had been a sacrifice on her part. She had not known she was to sacrifice their marriage.

Thinking of this, today, when everything seemed to be happening, thinking that even in the time he spent with Calhoun, he had made more decisions, he wondered when it would end. What more did the day hold for him? He had not known when he came in here that he would never again sleep in the same bed, in the same house with his wife. He had not known either that Lucinda must resign immediately—a two-week vacation to make it seem natural, but do it today. Yet he would go to her tonight—of that he was certain, and suddenly he needed her now. To sit and talk, merely that. And he wondered how it had come to be that she meant so much to him.

And Virgil. He had fucked him over but good. His vengeance was complete or would be when Max Calhoun made his telephone call. Yet he felt no pleasure. Nor did he feel remorse. But he did wonder how and where he learned to be so coldly vindictive. He called for another drink.

It happened then, way back in Los Caballos. A cold cold morning and a very hot mid-day. Eating his breakfast, sitting on the cold, hard clay which was the floor. His greatgrandfather came and sat down. His greatgrandmother had died a few days ago and he came to eat with them. Campeche slinked to a corner when he saw him. Even the dog was afraid of the greatgrandfather. The old man wanted his eggs but there were no eggs. "¿Que las gallinas ya no ponen?" he asked. "Se los tragó el perro," said his grandmother, and he was so frightened that he could not eat his food. "¡Campeche!" said his greatgrandfather in a strong voice, and the dog came toward him slowly with fear in his face and did not come too close, but his greatgrandfather did not hit him. He just said, "Al ratito me la pagas, perro hijo de la chingada." Then he said that he was going into town to bring a new woman for himself and said a name, and Ramón's grandfather said, "But that woman is big with child." And his greatgrandfather said, and he smiled, "When you buy a cow with calf, why the calf belongs to you, no?" Campeche did not join him in the prairie while he watched the cows that day, and he forgot about the dog even when he had locked the animals in the corral that evening; then he saw him hanging from the mesquite where his greatgrandfather had left him before he went to town so that the other dogs would be warned of what would happen to them if they stole eggs. He walked up to Campeche and he touched his body and it was hard.

SIXTEEN

Clemente Chacón paced the large living room, looking at the photographs of Evangeline's family as he always did when he came here. People now dead, every one of them, with the exception of Wanda, who might as well be dead since she had not been heard from in five years. In California she had been then, and a postcard from the beach at Santa Cruz had revealed to Evangeline that she was on her honeymoon with her third husband.

He had been shown into the house by a Mexican woman who came across the border every day to help Evangeline. This one he did not know. He had brought the first one because the house was much too large for Evangeline to take care of by herself, and although she lived alone, she would not leave this house, nor would she close up any part of it. He convinced her she should not live alone, so he brought a girl from Mexico with papers to stay with her, and then one day the girl had a baby and disappeared. One of the great frustrations of Evangeline's life was that she had been too dense to know. First she had not known the girl was pregnant until just before the child was born, then she had not expected her to slip away into the night two days after she had delivered in this very living room. Doña Rosa, who lived down the street—for now Mexicans were allowed to live in the neighborhood—had helped her with the girl, and when Evangeline saw the perfectly formed boy, she knew she wanted them to remain with her, the girl no longer a servant but a member of her family, for Evangeline had lost all her boys.

"The son of a bitch who got her in trouble in the first place probably has her in a dirty shack somewhere," she told Clemente. She had learned to talk like this from her George, although she had never used that language in his presence because it would have shocked him.

Clemente stopped before a picture of George Morgan in trooper's uniform, standing alongside a horse. At another table were two separate photographs of blond, almost identical young men in flight suits. He moved along the room where, at a larger table, arranged almost like an altar, were silver and gold cups and pictures of Charlie Morgan. He always looked at this display with emotion. Charlie standing in football uniform, muscular legs apart, the classic stance with helmet in one hand and a football in the other, his face not smiling, merely questioning; another of Charlie cutting back into the line, one on the diamond which caught him at the end of a swing of what was obviously a base hit. And Charlie in a track uniform, going over a last high hurdle; Charlie on a basketball court; and alongside the photographs was a football from a playoff game long ago, baseballs that had been home runs, pennants, and Clemente wondered why she did not throw these things away.

She entered the room, walking directly to him for her kiss. "How are you, son?" she asked.

"I'm alright, I guess," he answered like a little boy. "And you, Evangeline? How have you been?"

"Fair to middlin'," she answered, and they both knew the other lied. They looked at each other and she said, "I been having a pain—need a little operation, the Doc says. That's all. What's your problem?"

"Operation? For what?" His voice showed his concern.

"Tumor. He won't know how bad it is until it's out."

He decided he would talk to the doctor tomorrow.

She brought a decanter and glasses. "Have a little sherry with me and tell me what's troubling you."

"Do you have something else?" he asked.

She looked surprised, but moved to a cabinet and brought a bottle of bourbon. She went into the kitchen to get ice. "Tell me," she said.

"I found my wife with a man today. In our home. They were making love."

She felt for him and for herself, and reached out a hand to touch him. "Poor Clem," she said. "Poor, poor, Clem." She had always believed that he had been born for unhappiness because of his connection with her son. She had known about him long before the Senator brought him to her house because Charlie had written from Mexico. "Has this been going on some time?" she asked. "Could it have been only this once—this one time?"

"Just this one time, she said to me, but that is bad enough. Once is more than enough."

Evangeline Morgan moved and sat next to him. She seemed lost in thought while he did not speak. She asked, "Does she want to continue with this man? Is that what is troubling you most?"

"Christ, Evangeline!" he said. "She did a most terrible thing. That she did it, that is what is troubling me. That she did it, even if only once. That she would want to do it, even if she never did perform the act

142

would in itself be more than I could bear, don't you see? If she could have come to me and said, 'I have an irresistable desire for this man, I love him,' even if I could prevent anything happening—and I surely would try because I love her—I don't know if I could ever recover from it. I suppose in time I would, but I think of the years of unhappiness I would give her because that would always remain in my mind. I would suffer every day as I am suffering now. No, she does not want to continue with him, she loves me, and I believe her. In some crazy way she thinks she did this for me. But I must think of how it will be. I must think of the years ahead. How much will I make her suffer for her transgression. Even if she had not lain with him, even if she had only a desire to do so. How many thousands of nights would I fall asleep with the man in my mind? How many mornings would I waken to see the man in my mind's eye? And what would it do to her—to us? And how much of my suffering would I transfer to her? Or should I find myself a woman so that I could expiate her sin of merely having a desire for another man? And feel the pain rise from my groin upward to envelop me and constrict against my heart, nuturing hostility and rejection of that which I love most in life. From my groin, a fitting place to begin. And with my entire being burning with love, showing her only that part of me which hurt, through cruelty I could not control."

She asked, "Is it so terrible, then—so bad a thing that she did this? If you had never known about it, would it have made a difference?"

"Of course it would have. Don't ask me how, but it would have made a difference. It would make her different, and because of that it would make a difference to me." He placed his head in his hands and continued, "And because she did it for me, for my career, *she did it for money*, don't you see?"

She shook her head, but could not be truly angry. "And what?" she asked. "Why is that so wrong?"

"My God! You know what my mother was!"

"I know only what your mother *is*," she said, and now in anger. "She is a good woman, and she has suffered much. What you suffered in Mexico made you want to come here and better yourself, but she suffered much more than you ever did." Her voice softened. "You know," she said, "I have seen your mother and have a love for her."

"You've seen her? Why? And why haven't you told me?"

"You weren't told of it because you removed yourself from her. You judged her. To you she was or is a bad woman. You will not see her because she might hurt your career."

"It hasn't been only that."

"No, not only that. You don't think she is good enough to associate with your wife and child. Maybe what has happened is a good thing after all. At least you know people are human."

No, he thought, that wasn't all of it at all. No one knew the times, especially in the beginning, when he had to fight himself to keep from going to her. No one knew the feelings of guilt he had never completely repressed. And for what? Not for Queli, certainly not for Pete, but really because of the fear he had of being deported. He was also thinking now that he had not truly made a decision about Queli when he talked to Calhoun. That as of this moment he did not know what he would do, and that was why he had told Evangeline. All his life he dreaded the idea of being common; now what his wife had done made him like anyone else. He was also aware that in the end, she had done it for him. If he should get the Los Angeles office, would it not be a good trade-off? Ironic, but perhaps worth the pain.

She was saying, "You searched me out, you came to me and have looked out for me all these years because you loved my son. I saw your mother because she loved my son, has always loved him. Yes, and I saw her because I love you. She told me how my boy died. I was never sure that he was dead until she told me." She stopped talking and her face became even more pale. "I'm going to tell you something," she continued. "I am going to tell you this terrible, shameful thing because you were there when Charlie died, because it may help you now when your marriage seems to be falling apart and I want to help prevent this from happening. And, also, because I have always thought of you as my Charlie's son. In my mind and heart, I am your grandmother. Don't take that away from me."

He looked at her with tears in his eyes. "It *is* strange, but somehow I've always felt that Chale Morgan was my father. I suppose that is why I never called Mr. Chacón "father." Yet, I also thought of *him* as my father. I think I have always felt a sorrow for Chale Morgan."

"He deserved to be pitied," she said. "I know what my son was. The Senator told me some of it, as did your mother, even though she did not criticize him because she loved him. And the funny thing is, that you are more like my George than he ever was. It's almost as if you really have George's blood." She was pensive for a moment, then she spoke. "And I must tell you this—I really must, even though I never meant to let a soul know and I've lived alone with it these many years.

"It can happen to any woman as it can happen to a man. And sometimes, a person can't do a damned thing about it. I was unfaithful to

George once. One time! I know you can't believe it, seeing me, and knowing I'm eighty-three years old, but it happened, and I have never forgiven myself."

He looked at her and shook his head no, knowing her pain in having to divulge what should remain hidden. Knowing also that she could not even express that which she had done, but must say, *it happened*, because it was so shameful.

"You give me some of what you're drinking," she said suddenly. "I think I need a nip—a jolt, my George called it—to make this easier."

"You don't have to do it," he said. "You don't have to suffer for me. Leave it be." She merely looked at him and he brought her a drink.

"We were in Huachuca when it happened. A most terrible, isolated place. But that was the life of a trooper. The trooper and his family had to live in faraway deserts. And it happened when George was away on a bivouac—I guess it would have happened if he was only away for a few hours.

"The man was an officer—a special kind of officer, not regular calvary. He was special because the Army decided that the NCO club was fine for the troopers but didn't have nothing for their families. So this man arranged dances and family gatherings—even brought in some people to put on a marionette show for the kiddies. I remember George saying that the man was a fag. Maybe he was; he certainly talked and acted like a girl sometimes, but he was dangerous because all the ladies, me included, were definitely smitten by him. Thinking back, I wonder how many of the girls he got to. He was like one of us in a way, and kinda sneaked up on you. I don't even know after all this time how it happened. All I know is that he paid attention to all of us, and, you know, I thought I was the only one—that he paid special attention to me. He could make you feel that way. I still don't know how I came to do such a thing. But from the first, I just knew I wanted to love that man. I tol' myself later that it wouldn't a' happened if George had not gone away, sorta like blaming George, you see, but I was an Army wife, and I knew he had to do the things he had to do. Anyway, I wanted that man so much I couldn't sit still. I thought I must be crazy, but I wanted him. And it happened. It happened once. He came by the place in the middle of the day. It was natural. He always came to the house during the day to ask us wives for suggestions, wanting to know what kind of fun we could think up. I know now that I was waiting for him all morning. I was all cleaned up and scrubbed and I had a nice clean frock on—actually, I had never worn it—with nothing on underneath, can you believe that of me?—

and I knew that he would come. Well, he had his fun, alright, and me along with him. It happened only once," she repeated, "but that was enough.

"And when my George come back, I couldn't love him enough. I had never stopped loving him and I didn't love the other fellow, I just had to do it that's all. And I never told a soul about it. I lived with my guilt. At first it was mostly fear, and when Charlie was born, I wasn't afraid any more because I knew my George was the father. Don't ask me how I knew, women just know, that's all.

"All the time I was carrying Charlie, I was crazy with fear and maybe that's why Charlie turned out bad. But I always lived with my guilt. Even now, after my George has been dead these many years, I have my guilt, and I will carry it to my grave. And that is being crazy, you know?"

"Yes, I do know," said Clemente. "Despite the way I feel about my situation, I do know. And I can't control the way I feel."

"Because it didn't matter, except to me," she continued. "It was a terrible sin to me, but it did nothing to George."

"Because he didn't know," said Clemente.

"Because he didn't know, and because I loved him and knew that it could never happen again," said Evangeline.

"But you see, I *do* know," said Clemente. "And she does not feel guilt. And I don't know that she will never do it again. And the thing I do not know is, what am I to do about it?"

"I told you this; perhaps through the years I have had a need to tell someone. But I have also been hopin', wishing that it would help you. You're hurt, I know, and I hurt with you, but you belong with your wife. Forgive her."

He reached out a hand to her face. Then he took her hand. "I know what you are doing. And I have forgiven her, but I do not know if we can live together in the way we have. I find I have no desire for her; will I ever again? I fear I am psychologically castrated. I don't even know that I can do it with another woman. I must find out. I don't know." He poured another drink.

"You are still very Mexican, aren't you, my son?" she said this sadly. "But even though it makes me grieve that you should feel this way, I wouldn't want you to be like my Charlie was."

He looked at her in surprise.

"I told you I knew what my Charlie was," she said. "I know the kind of women he loved." She placed a hand on his arm. "I'm not talking about your mother, you must know. I have talked to her more than once.

146

I know her and she is good. What happened to her long ago was not her fault."

Clemente was suddenly angry again. "Who took you to see her?"

She accepted his anger. "The Senator took me," she said. "And later Leopoldo Smith took me whenever I asked him to do so. But why do you frown? Still because we didn't tell you? You didn't want to know, and if you did know, do you think you could stop me from doing it?"

Clemente was contrite. "I'm sorry, Evangeline. I'm finding out a great many things today that I didn't know. I feel as if people have been doing things behind my back." He stood up and walked to the window as was his habit. She walked up behind him.

"You can't do this to yourself," she said. "It just can't be this way. It's past now. You got to believe it's past and just go on." She put her thin arms around his waist and placed a cheek against his back. "You have to!" she said fiercely. He was all she had left, and he did not belong to her, was not of her. But his happiness could not be destroyed, and to her, his marriage was his happiness.

"Here comes a cab," he said. "It must be the Senator."

Driving into the center of the city with Porfirio Díaz, Clemente said, "She told you, didn't she?"

"About the operation?"

"About me."

"Yes."

Clemente was beyond being angry. He was bewildered. "¿Pero qué tienen todos ustedes conmigo? Como si yo fuera un escuincle." And he realized he had said the same thing to Leopoldo.

"¿Cómo?"

"Minding my affairs. Taking her to see my mother. Everything."

The Senator placed a hand on his shoulder. "You must know we are not minding your affairs. You will do what you have to do. No one is telling you what to do except, of course, Evangeline. But she is old, and a woman, and she has lost her sons, her husband, and even her daughter. But you see we have a thing in common, every one of us—Evangeline, Leopoldo, your sister, your mother and me—yes, even your wife. We all love you. Can't you see how fortunate you are to be loved? Do you realize that when you were tending cows the only person who loved you was your mother, and later, on the street, nobody loved you. And now, even Virgil loves you."

147

"That's bullshit, and you know it."

"I believe he does. It's strange, but he does."

"And what did you decide I should do, you and Evangeline back there. I know she wants me to continue as if nothing had happened. Do you agree with her?"

The Senator was sad. "Not at all, although if you should do that it should be because it is the right thing for you."

"What do you want me to do?"

"I only want you to be true to yourself. To do what you believe you must do," said Porfirio Díaz.

"I don't know what I am," said Clemente.

"Yes you do. Perhaps it is too soon to come to a decision."

"What would you do?"

"Does that matter? I'm much older than you. And I have old ideas, yet I doubt I could hurt Virgil. After all, we have made some progress. We are more civilized than to kill the man that seduces our wife. But I don't believe I could see him again, could talk to him again. Certainly, I could never work for him."

Clemente drove very carefully because he was not calm. "You're disappointed in me," he said.

"Why? Because you didn't kill him, cut his balls off? No. You will do something about it; I only hope for your sake it is the right thing." The Senator seemed to be thinking of something else. "Remember, though, that when you need help, I'll be there," he said. He continued to speak softly, almost sadly. "I said those very words to someone a long time ago. To Chale Morgan. I was a young lawyer then, and I liked Chale very much because inside he was good. There were many things wrong with him but he was not cruel. I liked him for that. He never asked a favor from me until the end. I sent him the money to come North, and it caused his death."

"You sent him the money? I remember my mother always said his sister sent it to him."

"I sent it. And it was not a mistake to send it. My mistake was to trust in someone to pick him up."

"Lázaro López," said Clemente.

The Senator looked at him for a moment. "Of course you would know. You were there," he said. "I was crazy about sports, that's how I got to know Chale and Lázaro. They were both excellent athletes. The biggest thing this town had ever seen. And they were the closest of friends. Chale didn't even seem to try. He was a natural, but Lázaro worked very hard to excel. Almost proving that the role of the Chicano holds true in everything—he must work harder than the Anglo to make it in America. But he had the desire and determination, and the Cleveland Browns had a pair of running guards who didn't weigh over a hundred and ninety each, and that was what Lázaro wanted to be. The boys were both high school All-Americans in their senior year, and Lázaro took a scholarship at Boulder, played two games his first year and quit. He couldn't wait four years to begin to make money. He didn't want fame, he wanted money, so he went to work for those people across the river."

"And Chale?" asked Clemente.

"It was different for Chale because he was different. He was never concerned about money, perhaps because he never lacked it while he was growing up. That's why I liked him better than the other before he became what he was. Chale was being romanced by the entire Big Eight Conference in his senior year. Then he won the Most Valuable Player award in the high school All-Star game and became one of the most wanted high school athletes in the country. Austin sent word that he was not to play any other sport his last year. They did not want him hurt. They were certain he would enroll there. But Charlie had a secret. He wanted to go to West Point, and he would have gone. He wanted to do this for his dead father and also for his mother and perhaps because a Morgan had fought alongside George Washington. Well, they could keep him off competitive contact sports, but they couldn't keep him off the track, and he hurt a knee.

"That ended West Point although that did not necessarily have to be true. He simply lost interest. The colleges waited for the doctor's report after the operation and when the surgeon declared it negative, that was it. Yes, I set Chale up to be killed without even knowing it, but I feel no guilt. How could I have known that Lázaro would betray him. I think betrayal must be unexpected or else it isn't betrayal. He was coming home, Chale wrote me, to straighten out his life. He told me many things in that letter, but one thing I keep remembering is that he turned your mother back to prostitution so that he could love her more. He was a strange one."

Clemente was silent. The Senator had not helped him much, but he had at least turned his mind away from his problems by talking about Chale Morgan.

Mr. Smith sat at the head table. He had not been expected but had been in the air at the moment Clemente and Max Calhoun were having their talk. His brother would arrive tomorrow. Clemente sat at his right,

Queli alongside him, looking beautiful in a low-cut gown. He looked across the table, where the Senator sat with Cipriano Cantú, talking to him very seriously. Clemente almost smiled, thinking of how the student leader would take Porfirio Díaz' refusal to participate in the showdown tomorrow. He saw his new man, Villegas, looking distinguished, hair trimmed, and wearing a tuxedo. Alongside sat his wife, a small, extremely pretty woman. He could not see Virgil, but he had talked to him for a few minutes and felt no hostility. Around the room he saw civic leaders and leaders of the Chicano community. He knew Leopoldo Smith and Caridad were away from him on his side of the table, though he could not see them. He did not know that Leopoldo stared coldly and intensely at Cipriano Cantú.

Max Calhoun had introduced the mayor and the mayor was giving a short, political speech. Now Clemente realized that he was being introduced. Queli squeezed his arm hard as he stood up. He moved to the podium and applause reverberated in the banquet hall. He raised his hands and began to speak.

"Meestair Smeeth," he said. "Frans from the hom offeece y señoras y señores ... " He thought of Mario Carbajal and in his mind he rejoiced as he heard the spontaneous laughter. *He could play the game and he had really made the transition. And he knew what he would do.*

EPILOGUE

In Sun City, California, Virgil Smith sat in the breakfast nook, while his wife, happy that she could do something for him, prepared his Cream o' Wheat. He sat watching a surveyor's crew across the highway measuring a plot of ground.

"Goddamnit Agatha! I'm not going to sit here and watch those cocksuckers dig a hole to dump me in. I've got twenty years left in me, we both have, and here they're building a goddamned cemetery right across the street!"

"Well," said Mrs. Smith, "I can't do anything about it, dear."

"Yes you can," he said, "we all can. I've got a mind to call Del Webb and ask him why in the hell he didn't buy that property. This son of a bitch made millions in L.A. burying people, advertising on streetcars, buses and Goodyear dirigibles, for Christ Sake, and now he comes out here and builds a cemetery in the desert and I'm supposed to sit here and eat my breakfast, while I watch those bastards fix my grave? I got a good mind to go back to work—I retired early because I knew we could have everything here." And indeed they did. They had a lovely two-bedroom home with a fine yard, a park across the street, a community pool, a recreation center, churches of every denomination but not a synagogue, of course, a movie house which showed clean pictures, a nine-hole golf course, and facilities for dancing and bingo and contract bridge. But Virgil Smith did not expect this business of waking up every morning to contemplate his grave.

And they were all Caucasian here, at least until now, and the residents were up in arms about a Mexican named Cárdenas who had just bought a house down at the next cul de sac. They were unaware that he was also a Caucasian.

But Virgil Smith forgot about Cárdenas for now. "Christ, I once wrote up the whole Goddamn New York Yankee baseball team, even a blind relief pitcher named Rhyne Duren. Shit, Webb knows who I am and I'm gonna call him."

Mrs. Smith was now at her needlepoint. "Where is he, dear?"

"I don't know—New York, Oakland, Phoenix—yeah, probably. I understand he has another dump like this near there." He looked at his wife for a moment. And he felt a love for her he did not remember. "You know, Agatha," he said, as if it had never occurred to him, "You are really a pretty smart woman."

"A person would have to be to live with you, Virgil." And she smiled, rocking, for she was partial to rockers.

"And you know old Virgil Smith pretty goddamn well, don't you?"

"Yes, dear."

He looked at her with admiration. She kept herself youthful; he saw what he had rarely seen. She is still a fine piece, he thought, and his eyes widened and he said, "Damn, Agatha, you are still a fine-looking piece," and she smiled at him with love because she had never stopped loving him, knowing full well that he knew as she did that she had never been a good piece, and he said, because old people can be candid, "Agatha, why is it that we never once, in all these years, fucked in the daytime?"

"Because you never asked me, Virgil." She still rocked, and for the only time in their relationship, a trace of hidden bitterness revealed itself. "Perhaps if you had, things would not have been the same."

He was disturbed because he did not understand her meaning, but defensively became righteous, and thought, what the hell is she complaining about. I put it to her regular, four or five times a year, and I put it to her good, if I say so myself. And he did, not because either of them needed it but because she expected it.

"I can go for a little of that right now, Agatha," he said, standing up and scratching his groin, monkey-like.

"It's a little late in the day for that, Virgil."

"Don't ever again say I never offered, Agatha. And for Chrissakes, don't be a fractious old woman," said Virgil Smith.

In Washington, D.C., Porfirio Díaz, U. S. Senator, Junior, from the sovereign state of Texas, sipped a cordial and said, "Yes, Mr. President. You have my full support and cooperation. The Bracero problem and the problem of illegal Mexican Nationals can be settled with honest and intelligent dialogue. I feel honored to be your personal representative at the conference in Mexico." He had never expected to come this far but because of a quirk in the machinations of politics, he was in this position. And here he was, now married to the socialite widow of a career diplomat; he had removed the one remaining obstacle to political success, bachelorhood. He was now being talked of as a potential candidate for the Vice-Presidency, the proverbial heartbeat away, which he knew to be pure political rhetoric. It could never be for him. But as he walked out of the White House that evening, he walked with pride, tall in the saddle, because he was living proof of the fact that, although the founding fathers were not talking about Mexicans when they spoke of freedom and liberty and justice, one day, within his lifetime perhaps, a cholito, a nigger or a kike would be President of the United States. This was inevitable. And he laughed suddenly at the notion of a dark Mexican holding Tlaloc in the right hand and the stars and stripes in the other.

And somewhere in Los Angeles, a beautiful young woman drove a station wagon into the parking lot of an office building. She sat and watched him as he walked toward her, a little balder than when she had met him, and she felt that familiar constriction in her chest she always felt when he returned to her, for he was not only her husband but her salvation.

He kissed her briefly, then walked around to climb in beside her.

"Vengo más cansao que la chingada," he said.

"I'll fix your tub as soon as we get home."

She drove carefully and as she shifted gears at an intersection, he reached under her arm for her breast. "I don' wanna bath," he said exaggerating his speech. "Jes wanna lay down between your legs for about a half-hour an' rest."

She laughed. "That's not resting. And you know, I worked for you for almost three years and didn't know you had such appetites."

"I didn't know it either," he said. And they both laughed.

"What's new?" he asked.

"Good things first?"

"OK."

"Well," she said. "Phillips Exeter decided Pete can benefit from their brand of education. And I found a beautiful roast for only four dollars a pound."

"What's bad?"

"Little Leo has come down with something. I'm calling the doctor as soon as we get home. Temperature's pretty high."

"I don't trust that Messican doctor. We ought to get another."

She laughed silently. "He's good. One of the best, and he delivered both kids."

"OK," he said. "He's the best doctor in the worl'—but..."

In the child's bedroom, he took one look and his body shook. "Forget Dr. Cadena," he said. "Has anyone been here today?"

She looked at the child and one side of his face seemed paralyzed, the eye not closed but seemingly smaller than the other.

"Why yes," she said. "The new people up the lane."

"Did they touch him?"

"No. They just stood at the door admiring him, why?"

"Call Leopoldo," he said. "Tell him his godson has mal de ojo. He can be here by morning."

"What is this? Why shouldn't I call Dr. Cadena?"

"He can't do anything for Leo. That's why. I'll be back as quickly as I can."

"But where are you going? The roast is nearly done!"

"Fuck the roast! I'm going to the East Side. And pray that I can find a Mexican woman who knows about these things."